Praise for *New York Times* and *USA TODAY* bestselling author RaeAnne Thayne

"Romance, vivid characters and a wonderful story; really, who could ask for more?"
—Debbie Macomber, #1 *New York Times* bestselling author, on *Blackberry Summer*

"Entertaining, heart-wrenching, and totally involving, this multithreaded story overflows with characters readers will adore."
—*Library Journal*

"This holiday-steeped romance overflows with family and wintry small-town appeal."
—*Library Journal* on *Snowfall on Haven Point*

"A sometimes heartbreaking tale of love and relationships in a small Colorado town.... Poignant and sweet."
—*Publishers Weekly* on *Christmas in Snowflake Canyon*

"This quirky, funny, warmhearted romance will draw readers in and keep them enthralled to the last romantic page."
—*Library Journal* on *Christmas in Snowflake Canyon*

"RaeAnne Thayne is quickly becoming one of my favorite authors.... Once you start reading, you aren't going to be able to stop."
—*Fresh Fiction*

"RaeAnne has a knack for capturing those emotions that come from the heart."
eviews

"Her engaging   rom the very first pa

d Road

Dear Reader,

This is my sixteenth book in the overarching The Cowboys of Cold Creek series (which is really a collection of various miniseries within a series). Every time I tell myself I'm done with the series, I come up with one more idea, another character I can't leave hanging. The moment I introduced Ella Baker in last year's *The Holiday Gift*, I knew I would have to tell her story. She played an important role in that book by helping the hero and heroine finally come together, but in the process, Ella ended up with her heart bruised. I couldn't let that be the end of things for her! I'm thrilled to have the chance to give the earnest and caring music teacher her own happy ending with sexy rancher Beckett McKinley—and his unruly twin boys!

Every time I return to Pine Gulch, I feel like I'm back among friends. Thank you for coming along!

Wishing you all the most joyous of holidays!

RaeAnne

RaeAnne Thayne

THE RANCHER'S CHRISTMAS SONG

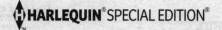

HARLEQUIN® SPECIAL EDITION®

Recycling programs
for this product may
not exist in your area.

ISBN-13: 978-0-373-62380-8

The Rancher's Christmas Song

Copyright © 2017 by RaeAnne Thayne

Printed in U.S.A.

www.Harlequin.com

RaeAnne Thayne finds inspiration in the beautiful northern-Utah mountains, where the *New York Times* and *USA TODAY* bestselling author lives with her husband and three children. Her books have won numerous honors, including RITA® Award nominations from Romance Writers of America and a Career Achievement Award from *RT Book Reviews*. RaeAnne loves to hear from readers and can be contacted through her website, www.raeannethayne.com.

Books by RaeAnne Thayne

Harlequin Special Edition

The Cowboys of Cold Creek

The Holiday Gift
A Cold Creek Christmas Story
The Christmas Ranch
A Cold Creek Christmas Surprise
A Cold Creek Noel
A Cold Creek Reunion
Christmas in Cold Creek
A Cold Creek Baby
A Cold Creek Secret
A Cold Creek Holiday
A Cold Creek Homecoming
The Cowboy's Christmas Miracle
Dalton's Undoing

HQN Books

Haven Point

Serenity Harbor
Snowfall on Haven Point
Riverbend Road
Evergreen Springs
Redemption Bay
Snow Angel Cove

For a complete list of books by RaeAnne Thayne, please visit www.raeannethayne.com.

To my dad, Elden Robinson,
who loved Westerns and cowboy music and
who made the best popcorn west of the Mississippi.
I miss you more than words can say.

Chapter One

The twin terrors were at it again.

Ella Baker watched two seven-year-old tornadoes, otherwise known as Trevor and Colter McKinley, chase each other behind the stage curtains at the Pine Gulch Community Center.

In the half hour since they arrived at the community center with their father, they had spilled a water pitcher, knocked down a life-size cardboard Santa and broken three ornaments on the big Christmas tree in the corner.

Now they were racing around on the stage where tonight's featured act was set to perform within the next half hour.

She would have to do something. As organizer and general show-runner of this fund-raising event for the school's underfinanced music program, it was her responsibility to make sure everyone had a good time.

People's wallets tended to open a little wider when they were happy, comfortable and well fed. A gang of half-pint miscreants had the potential to ruin the evening for everyone.

She had tried to talk to them. As usual, the twins had offered her their angelic, gap-toothed smiles and had promised to behave, then moments later she saw them converge with four other boys to start playing this impromptu game of tag on the stage.

In order to tame these particular wild beasts, she was going to have to talk to someone in authority. She gave a last-ditch, desperate look around. As she had suspected, neither their uncle nor their great uncle was in sight. That left only one person who might have any chance of corralling these two little dynamos.

Their father.

Ella's stomach quivered. She did *not* enjoy talking to Beck McKinley and avoided it as much as possible.

The man made her so ridiculously nervous. He always treated her with careful politeness, but she could never read the expression on his features. Every time she spoke with him—which was more often than she liked, considering his ranch was next door to her father's—she always felt like she came out of the encounter sounding like a babbling fool.

Okay, yes. She was attracted to him, and had been since she moved back to Pine Gulch. What woman wouldn't be? Big, tough, gorgeous, with a slow smile that could charm even the most hardened heart.

She didn't *want* to be so drawn to him, especially when he hadn't once shown a glimmer of interest in return. He made her feel like she was an awkward teenager back in private school in Boston, holding up the wall at her first coed dance.

She wasn't. She was a twenty-seven-year-old professional in charge of generating funds for a cause she cared about. Sexy or not, Beck had to corral his sons before they ruined the entire evening.

Time to just suck it up and take care of business. She was a grown-up and could handle talking to anyone, even big, tough, stern-faced ranchers who made her feel like she didn't belong in Pine Gulch.

It wasn't hard to find Beck McKinley. He towered about four inches taller than the crowd of ranchers he stood among.

She sucked in a steadying breath and made her way toward the group, trying to figure out a polite way to tell him his sons were causing trouble again.

She wasn't completely surprised to find her father was part of the group around Beck. They were not only copresidents of the local cattle growers association this year, but her father also idolized the man. As far as Curt Baker was concerned, Beck McKinley was all three wise men rolled into one. Her father still relied heavily on Beck for help—more so in the last few years, as his Parkinson's disease grew more pronounced and his limitations more frustrating.

At least her father was sitting down, leaning slightly forward with his trembling hands crossed in front of him atop the cane she had insisted he bring.

He barely looked at her, too engrossed in the conversation about cattle prices and feed shortages.

She waited until the conversation lagged before stepping into the group. She was unwilling to call out the rancher over his troublemaking twins in front of all the others.

"Beckett. May I have a brief word?"

His eyebrows rose and he blinked in surprise a few times. "Sure. Excuse me, gentlemen."

Aware of curious gazes following them, Ella led Beck a short distance from his peers.

"Is there a problem?" he asked.

She pointed toward the pack of wild boys on the stage, who were chasing each other between the curtains. "Your sons are at it again."

His gaze followed her gesture and he grimaced. "I see half a dozen boys up there. Last I checked, only two of those are mine."

"Colter and Trevor are the ringleaders. You know they are. They're always the ones who come up with the mischief and convince the others to go along."

"They're natural leaders. Are you suggesting I try to put the brakes on that?"

His boys were adorable, she had to admit, but they were the bane of her existence as the music teacher at Pine Gulch Elementary School. They couldn't sit still for more than a few minutes at a time and were constantly talking to each other as well as the rest of the students in their class.

"You could try to channel it into more positive ways."

This wasn't the first time she had made this suggestion to him and she was fairly certain she wasn't the only educator to have done so. Trevor and Colter had been causing problems at Pine Gulch Elementary School since kindergarten.

"They're boys. They've got energy. It comes with the package."

She completely agreed. That was one of the reasons she incorporated movement in her music lessons with all of her students this age. All children—but especially boys, she had noticed—couldn't sit still for long hours at a time and it was cruel to expect it of them.

She was a trained educator and understood that, but she also expected that excess energy to be contained when necessary and redirected into proper behavior.

"Our performers will be taking the stage soon. Please, can you do something with the boys? I can just picture them accidentally ripping down the curtains or messing with the lights before we can even begin."

Beck glanced at his boys, then back down at her. His strong jaw tightened, and in his eyes, she saw a flash of something she couldn't read.

She didn't need to interpret it. She was fairly certain she knew what he thought of her. Like her father, Beck thought she was a soft, useless city girl.

Both of them were wrong about her, but nothing she did seemed to convince them otherwise. As far as her father was concerned, she belonged in Boston or New York, where she could attend the symphony, the ballet, art gallery openings.

Since the moment she'd arrived here with her suitcases a little more than a year ago, Curt had been trying relentlessly to convince her to go back to Boston with her mother and stepfather and the cultured life they had.

Beck seemed to share her father's views. He never seemed to want to give her the time of day and always seemed in a big hurry to escape her presence.

Whatever his true opinion, he always treated her with stiff courtesy. She would give him that. Beck McKinley was never rude to anybody—probably one of the reasons all the other ranchers seemed to cluster around the man in public. Everybody seemed to respect his opinion and want to know what he had to say about things.

The only thing she wanted from him right now was to keep his boys from ruining the night.

"I'll talk to the parents of the other boys, too. I'm just asking if you'll please try to round up Colter and Trevor and have them take their seats. I'll be introducing our performers in a moment and I would like people to focus on what they came for, instead of how many straws Colter can stick up his nose."

He unbent enough to offer that rare, delicious smile. It appeared for only a moment. His cheeks creased and his eyes sparkled and his entire face looked even more gorgeous. "Good point, I suppose. The answer is five, in case you wanted to know. I'll grab them. Sorry they caused a ruckus."

"Thank you," she said, then walked away before she was tempted to make another joke, if only to see if he would offer up that smile again.

Better to quit while she was ahead, especially since her brain was now struggling to put together any words at all.

Beck watched Ella Baker walk away, her skirt swishing and her boot heels clicking on the old wooden floor of the community center.

He had the same reaction to her that he always did—sheer, wild hunger.

Something about that sleek blond hair and her almond-shaped eyes and the soft, kissable mouth did it to him. Every. Single. Time.

What was the *matter* with him? Why did he have to

be drawn to the one woman in town who was totally wrong for him?

Ella wore tailored skirts and suede boots that probably cost as much as a hand-tooled saddle. She was always perfectly put together, from the top of her sleek blond hair to the sexy but completely impractical shoes she always wore.

When he was around her, he always felt exactly like what he was—a rough-edged cowboy.

Can you at least pretend you have a little culture? Do you have any idea how hard it is to be married to someone who doesn't know Manet from Monet?

Though it had been four years since she died—and five since she had lived with him and the twins—Stephanie's words and others she had uttered like them seemed to echo through his memory. They had lost their sting over the years, but, boy, had they burned at the time.

He sighed. Though the two had similar blue-blood backgrounds and educations, Ella Baker looked nothing like his late wife. Stephanie had been tall, statuesque, with red hair she had passed on to their sons. Ella was slim, petite and looked like an exotic blonde fairy.

Neither of them fit in here, though he had to admit Ella tried a hell of a lot harder than Stephanie ever had. She had organized this event, hadn't she?

He should probably stop staring at her. He would. Any moment now.

Why did she have to be so damn beautiful, bright and cheerful and smiling? Every time he saw her, it was like looking into the sun.

He finally forced himself to look away so he could do as she asked, quite justifiably. He should have been keeping a better eye on the boys from the beginning, but he'd been sucked into a conversation about a new ranching technique his friend Justin Hartford was trying and lost track of them.

As he made his way through the crowd, smiling at neighbors and friends, he was aware of how alone he was. He had been bringing the boys to these community things by himself for nearly five years now. He could hardly believe it.

He was ready to get out there and date again. The boys had somehow turned seven, though he had no idea how that happened.

The truth was, he was lonely. He missed having someone special in his life. He was tired of only having his uncle and his brothers to talk to.

Heaven knows, he was really tired of sleeping alone.

When he did jump back into that whole dating arena, though, he was fairly sure it wouldn't be with a soft, delicate music teacher who didn't know a mecate from a bosal.

It might be easier to remember that if the woman wasn't so darned pretty.

In short order, he found the boys on the stage and convinced all of them it was time to find their parents and take their seats, then led his own twins out of trouble.

"Hey, Dad. Guess what Thomas said?" Colter asked, as they were making their way through the crowd.

"What's that, son?" He couldn't begin to guess what another seven-year-old might pass along—and was a little afraid to ask.

"His dog is gonna have puppies right before Christmas. Can we get one? Can we?"

He did his best not to roll his eyes at the idea. "Thomas and his family have a miniature Yorkie that's no bigger than my hand. I'm not sure a little dog like that would like living on a big ranch like ours with all our horses and cattle. Besides, we've already got three dogs. And one of those is going to have her own puppies any day now."

"Yeah, but they're *your* dogs. And you always tell us they're not pets, they're working dogs," Trevor said.

"And you told us we probably can't keep any of Sal's puppies," Colter added. "We want a puppy of our very own."

Like they didn't have enough going right now. He was not only running his horse and cattle ranch, the Broken Arrow, but also helping out Curt Baker at his place as much as possible. He had help from his brother and uncle, yeah—on the ranch and with the boys. He still missed his longtime housekeeper and nanny, Judy Miller, who was having double–knee replacement and would be out for six months.

Adding a little indoor puppy into the chaos of their life right now was completely unthinkable.

"I don't think that's going to happen," he said firmly but gently.

"Maybe Santa Claus will bring us one," Colter said, nudging his brother.

At seven, the boys were pretty close to understanding the truth about Santa Claus, though they had never come right out and told them. Every once in a while he thought they might know, but were just trying to hang on to the magic as long as possible. He was okay with that. Life would be full of enough disappointments.

He was saved from having to answer them by the sight of beautiful Ella Baker approaching the microphone.

"Hey! There's Miss Baker," Trevor said, loudly enough that she heard and looked in their direction.

Though families had been encouraged to attend the event and it was far from a formal concert, Beck was still embarrassed by the outburst.

"Shh," he said to the boys. "This is a time to listen, not talk."

"Like church?" Colter asked, with some measure of distrust.

"Sort of." *But more fun*, he thought, though of course he couldn't say to impressionable boys.

Trevor and Colter settled into their seats and Beck watched as Ella took the microphone. He figured he could watch her here without guilt, since everyone else's eyes were on her, too.

"Welcome, everyone, to this fund-raiser for the music program at the elementary and middle schools. By your presence here, it's clear you feel strongly about supporting the continued success of music education in our schools. As you know, programs like ours are constantly under the budget knife. Through your generous donations, we can continue the effort to teach music to the children of Pine Gulch. At this time, it's my great pleasure to introduce our special guests, all the way from northern Montana. Please join me in welcoming J. D. Wyatt and his Warbling Wranglers."

The introduction was met with a huge round of applause for the cowboy singers. Beck settled into his chair and prepared to savor the entertainment—and prayed it could keep his wild boys' attention.

He shouldn't have worried. An hour later, the band wrapped up with a crowd-pleasing, toe-tapping version of "Jingle Bell Rock" that had people getting up to dance in the aisle and in front of the small stage.

His twins had been utterly enthralled, from the first notes to the final chord.

"That was awesome!" Colter exclaimed.

"Yeah!" His twin glowed, as well. "Hey, Dad! Can we take fiddle lessons?"

Over the summer, they had wanted to learn to play the guitar. Now they wanted to learn the violin. Tomorrow, who knows, they might be asking for accordion lessons.

"I don't know. We'll have to see," he said.

Before the twins could press him, Ella Baker returned to the mic stand.

"Thank you all again for your support. Please remember all proceeds from ticket sales for tonight's performance, as well as our silent auction, will go toward funding music in the schools. Also, please don't forget tomorrow will be the first rehearsal for the Christmas show and dinner put on by the children of our community for our beloved senior citizens at The Christmas Ranch in Cold Creek Canyon. This isn't connected to the school and is completely voluntary. Any students ages four to sixteen are encouraged to join us."

"Hey. That's us!" Trevor said.

"Can we do it, Dad?" Colter asked, with the same pleading look on his face he wore when asking for a second scoop of ice cream. "We wanted to last year, remember? Only you said we couldn't because we were going to visit our Grandma Martin."

That had been a short-lived visit with Stephanie's mother in Connecticut, who had thought she would enjoy taking the boys into the city over the holidays and showing off her grandsons to her friends. After three days, she had called him to pick up the boys ahead of schedule, sounding ages older than she had days earlier. She hadn't called again this year.

"Can we?" Trevor persisted.

Beck didn't know how to answer as items on his massive to-do list seemed to circle around him like buzzards on a carcass. He had so much to do this time of year and didn't know how he could run the boys to and from the rehearsals at The Christmas Ranch, which was a good fifteen minutes away.

On the other hand, Ella Baker lived just next door. Maybe he could work something out with her to give the boys a ride.

Of course, that meant he would have to talk to her again, though. He did his best to avoid situations that put them into closer proximity, where he might be tempted to do something stupid.

Like ask her out.

"Please," Colter begged.

This was a good cause, a chance to reinforce to them the importance of helping others. The holiday show had become a high point to many of the senior citizens in town, and they looked forward to it all year. If the twins wanted to do it, how could he possibly refuse?

"We'll see," he hedged, not quite ready to commit.

"You always say that," Trevor said. "How come we never really *see* anything after you say we will?"

"Good question. Maybe someday, I'll answer it. We'll have to see."

The boys laughed, as he hoped, and were distracted by their friend Thomas—he, of the tiny puppies—who came over to talk to them.

"Are you gonna do the Christmas show? My mom said I could, if I wanted."

"We want to," Trevor said, with another cajoling look at Beck.

"Maybe we can have a band," Thomas said. "I'll be J.D. and you can be the Warbling Wranglers."

As they squabbled good-naturedly about which of them would make the better lead singer, Beck listened to them with a sense of resignation. If they really wanted to be in the Christmas program, he would have to figure out a way to make it happen—even if it meant talking to Ella Baker again.

The thought filled him with far more anticipation than he knew was good for him.

Chapter Two

"What a fantastic event!" Faith Brannon squeezed Ella's hand. "I haven't enjoyed a concert so much in a long time."

"Maybe that's because you never go out," Faith's younger sister, Celeste, said with a laugh.

"Newlyweds. What are you going to do?" Hope, the third Nichols sister, winked at their group of friends.

Ella had to laugh, even as she was aware of a little pang. Faith had married her neighbor, Chase Brannon, about four months earlier, in a lovely wedding in the big reception hall of The Christmas Ranch.

It had been lovely and understated, since it was a second marriage for both, but there hadn't been a dry eye in the hall. They seemed so in love and so deserving of happiness.

Ella had managed to smile all evening long. She considered that quite an accomplishment, considering once upon a time, she had completely made a fool of herself over the groom. When she first moved to Pine Gulch, she'd had a gigantic crush on Chase and had all but thrown herself at him, with no clue that he had adored Faith forever and had just been biding his time until she came to terms with her husband's premature death.

Ella had almost gotten over her embarrassment about events of the previous Christmas. It might have been easier to avoid the happy couple altogether except the Nichols sisters—all married now and with different surnames but still "the Nichols sisters" to just about everyone in town—had become some of her dearest friends.

They were warm and kind and always went out of their way to include her in activities.

"You did a great job of organizing," Hope said now. "I couldn't believe all the people who showed up. I met a couple earlier who drove all the way up from Utah because they love J.D. and his Wranglers. I hope you raked in the dough."

"Everyone has been generous," she said. "We should have enough to purchase the new piano we need in the elementary school with plenty left over for sheet music at the middle school."

She still didn't think it was right that the art and music programs had to struggle so much to make ends meet in this rural school system. Judging by tonight, though, many members of the community seemed to agree with her that it should be a priority and had donated accordingly.

"It was a great community event. What a great turnout!"

"Just think." Hope grinned. "We get to turn around

and do this again in a few weeks at The Christmas Ranch."

Faith made a face. "You wouldn't believe how many people have brought up that Christmas program to me tonight, and I'm not even involved in the show!"

"You're a Nichols, though, which makes you one of the co-queens of Christmas, like it or not," Ella said.

The Nichols family had been running The Christmas Ranch—a holiday-themed attraction filled with sleigh rides, a life-size Christmas village and even their own herd of reindeer—for many years. It was enormously successful and attracted visitors from around the region.

The popularity of the venue had grown exponentially in the last few years because of the hard work of the sisters.

A few years earlier, they had come up with the idea of providing a free catered dinner and holiday-themed show presented by area children as a gift to the local senior citizens and the event had become legendary in the community.

"We are so lucky that you've agreed to help us again this year," Celeste said now to Ella.

"Are you kidding? I've been looking forward to it all year."

The event—more like an old-fashioned variety show—wasn't professionally staged, by any means. Rehearsals didn't even start until a few weeks before the performance and there were no auditions and few soloists, but the children had fun doing it and the attendees enjoyed every moment.

The previous year's performance had been a wonderful growing experience for Ella, serving as an icebreaker of sorts to help her get to know the local children better.

She hoped this year would only build on that success.

"Wait until you see some of the songs we have planned. It's going to knock your socks off," she said.

"How can you be so excited about wrestling seventy schoolchildren already on a Christmas sugar high?" Faith shook her head. "You must be crazy."

"The very best kind of crazy," Celeste said with a smile.

"You fit right in with the rest of us," Hope assured her, then changed the subject. "Hey, did you see that good-looking guy who came in with Nate and Emery Cavazos? His name is Jess Saddler and he's temporarily staying at their cabins. Em said he's single and looking to move in and open a sporting goods store in town. He's cute, isn't he?"

She followed the direction of Hope's gaze and discovered a man she didn't know speaking with Nate and Emery, as well as Caroline and Wade Dalton. Hope was right, he was great-looking, with an outdoorsy tan and well-styled, sun-streaked hair that looked as if it had never seen a Stetson.

He also had that overchiseled look of people who earned their strength at the gym instead of through hard, productive manual labor.

"I suppose."

"You should go introduce yourself," Hope suggested, ignoring the sudden frown from both of her sisters.

"Why?" Ella asked, suspicious.

Hope's innocent shrug didn't fool her. "He's single. You're single. Em said he seems like a great guy and, I don't know, I thought maybe the two of you would hit it off."

"Are you matchmaking for me?"

"Do you want me to?" Hope asked eagerly.

Did she? She wasn't sure how to answer. Yes, she was lonely. It was tough to be a single woman in this family-oriented community, where everyone seemed paired up. There weren't very many eligible men to even date and she often felt isolated and alone.

She wasn't sure how she felt about being the latest pity project of her friends. Did she seem desperate to them?

That was an uncomfortable thought.

"I don't need a matchmaker. I'm fine," she told Hope. "Even if I met the right guy today, I'm not sure I would have time for him, between working at two schools, doing music therapy at the senior citizen center and taking my dad to doctor appointments."

"When you care about a man, you make time," Celeste said.

"I don't think the guy is going anywhere. After Christmas, you should think about it," Hope added.

"Maybe." She could only hope a bland nonanswer would be enough for them.

Hope looked disappointed but was distracted when another neighbor came up and asked her a question about a private company party scheduled the following week at The Christmas Ranch.

While she was occupied, Faith turned to Ella with a frown on her soft, pretty features.

"It sounds like you have too much on your plate," Faith said. "Now I feel guilty we roped you into doing the Christmas show again."

"You didn't rope me into anything," she assured her. "I meant what I said. I've been looking forward to it."

"When will you have time to breathe?"

She didn't mind being busy and loved teaching music.

It had been her passion through her teen years and pursuing a career in music therapy was a natural fit. She had loved her job before she came here, working at a school for students with developmental disabilities, but there was nothing like that here in this small corner of southeastern Idaho. Teaching music in the schools was the next best thing. She had to do something with her time, especially considering her father continued being completely stubborn and unreasonable about letting her take over the ranch.

She was busy. She just wasn't *that* busy.

"If you want the truth," she admitted, "I may have slightly exaggerated my overloaded schedule to keep Hope from making me her next project."

Faith looked amused. "Very wise move on your part."

"Don't get me wrong. It's sweet of her and everything. It's just…"

"You don't have to explain to me. I totally get it."

"I'm just not looking for a male right now."

"Too bad. Looks like a couple of cute ones are headed this way."

She followed Faith's gaze to find the twin terrors barreling straight toward her at full speed. To her relief, they managed to stop inches from knocking her and Faith over like bowling pins.

"Hey, Miss Baker. Miss Baker! Guess what?"

The boys' faces were both covered in chocolate, a fairly solid clue that they'd been raiding the refreshments table. How many cookies had they consumed between the pair of them? Not her problem, she supposed. Their father could deal with their upset stomachs and sugar overload.

"What's that, Trevor?" She directed her question to the one who had spoken.

He hid a grin behind his hand. "I'm not Trevor. I'm Colter."

"Are you sure?" She raised an eyebrow.

He giggled. "How come we can never fool you? You're right. I'm Trevor."

The boys were the most identical twins Ella had ever seen and they delighted in playing those kind of switch-up games with the faculty and staff at the elementary school. From the first time they met, though, Ella had never struggled to tell them apart. Colter had a slightly deeper cleft in his chin and Trevor had a few more freckles.

"Guess what?" Colter finished his brother's sentence. "We're gonna be in your Christmas show."

Beside her, Faith gave a small but audible groan that completely mirrored Ella's sudden panic.

On the heels of that initial reaction, she felt suddenly protective of the boys, defensive on their behalf. It really wasn't their fault they misbehaved. None of it was malicious. They were high-spirited in the first place and had a father who seemed more interested in taking over her father's ranch than teaching his two boys to behave like little gentlemen.

But then, she might be a tad biased against the man. Every time she offered to do something to help Curtis, her father was quick to tell her Beck would take care of it.

"Is that right?" she asked. The show was open to any children who wanted to participate, with no auditions and guaranteed parts for all. They wouldn't win any talent competitions, but she considered the flaws and scenery mishaps all part of the charm.

"Our dad said *we'll see*," Colter informed her. "Some-times that means no, but then I heard him asking your dad if he thought you might be able to give us a ride to and from practice on the days no one from the ranch could do it."

Her jaw tightened. The nerve of the arrogant rancher, to go to her father instead of asking her directly, as if Curt had any control over the matter.

"And what did my father say?"

"We didn't hear," Trevor confessed. "But can you?"

Their ranch was right next door to the Baker's Dozen. It would be no great hardship for her to accommodate the McKinleys and transport the twins if they wanted to participate, but it would be nice if Beck could be bothered asking her himself.

"I'll have to talk to your father first," she hedged.

The boys seemed to take her equivocation as the next best thing to a done deal.

"This will be fun," Colter said, showing off his gaptoothed grin. "We're gonna be the best singers you ever saw."

To reinforce the point, Trevor launched into a loud version of "Rudolph the Red-Nosed Reindeer" and his brother joined in. They actually had surprisingly good singing voices. She'd noticed that before during music class at school—though it was hard to confirm that now when they were singing at the tops of their lungs.

They were drawing attention, she saw. The cute guy with Em and Nate was looking this way and so was Beck McKinley.

Ella flushed, envisioning the nightmare of trying to keep the boys from trying to ride the reindeer at The Christmas Ranch, or from knocking down the gigantic sixteen-foot-tall tree inside the St. Nicholas Lodge.

"You can be in the show on one condition," she said, using her best teacher's voice.

"What's that?" Colter asked warily.

"Children of all ages will be participating, even some kindergarten students and first graders. They're going to need someone to set a good example about how to listen and pay attention. They'll be watching you. Can you show them the correct way to behave?"

"Yeah!" Trevor exclaimed. "We can be quiet as dead mice."

That was pretty darn quiet—and she would believe *that* when she saw it.

"We can be the goodest kids in the whole place," Colter said. "You'll see, Miss Baker. You won't even know we're there, except when we're singing."

"Yeah. You'll see," Trevor said. "Thanks, Miss Baker. Come on, Colt. Let's go tell Thomas." In a blink, the two of them raced off as quickly as they had appeared by her side.

"Those boys are quite a pair, aren't they?" Faith said, watching after them with a rather bemused look on her features.

Ella was again aware of that protective impulse, the urge to defend them. Yes, they could be exhausting but she secretly admired their take-no-prisoners enthusiasm for life.

"They're good boys. Just a little energetic."

"You can say that again. They're a handful. I suppose it's only to be expected, though." Faith paused, her expression pensive. "You know, I thought for sure Beck would send them off to live with family after their mother left. I mean, here was this tough, macho rancher trying to run his place while also dealing with a couple of boys still in diapers. The twins couldn't have been more than two."

"So young? How could a mother leave her babies?"

"Yeah. I wanted to chase after her and smack her hard for leaving a good man like Beck, but he would never let anybody say a bad word about her. The only thing he ever said to me was that Stephanie was struggling with some mental health issues and needed a little time to get her head on straight. I think she had some postpartum depression and it probably didn't help that she didn't have a lot of friends here. We tried, but she wasn't really very approachable."

Faith made a face. "That sounds harsh, doesn't it? That's not what I mean. She was just not from around here."

"Neither am I," Ella pointed out.

"Yes, but you don't constantly remind us of how much better things were back east."

Because they weren't. Oh, she missed plenty of things about her life there, mostly friends and neighbors and really good clam chowder, but she had always felt as if she had a foothold in two places—her mother's upper-crust Beacon Hill society and her father's rough-and-rugged Idaho ranch.

"Anyway, she left to get her head on straight when the boys were about two and I can't imagine how hard it must have been for Beck on his own. A year later, Stephanie died of a drug overdose back east."

"Oh, how sad. Those poor boys."

"I know. Heartbreaking. Her parents are high-powered doctors. They fought for custody of the boys and I think it got pretty ugly for a while, but Beck wouldn't hear of it. He's a good dad. Why would any judge take the boys away from father and the only home they've ever known and give them to a couple of strangers?"

"He strikes me as a man who holds on to what he considers his."

"That might have been part of it. But the truth is, Beckett adores his boys. You should have seen him, driving to cattle sales and the feed store with two toddlers strapped in their car seats in the crew cab of his pickup truck."

Her heart seemed to sigh at the picture. She could see it entirely too clearly, the big, tough rancher and his adorable carbon-copy twins.

"He's a good man," Faith said. "A woman could do far worse than Beckett McKinley. If you're ever crazy enough to let Hope fix you up, you shouldn't discount Beck on account of those wild boys of his."

That wouldn't be the only reason she could never look seriously at Beck, if she was in the market for a man—which she so totally wasn't. For one thing, she became nervous and tongue-tied around him and couldn't seem to string together two coherent thoughts. For another, the man clearly didn't like her. He treated her with a cool politeness made all the more striking when she saw his warm, friendly demeanor around others. And, finally, she was more than a little jealous of his close relationship with her father. Curt treated his neighboring rancher like the son he'd never had, trusting him with far more responsibility than he would ever consider giving his own daughter. How could she ever get past that?

She was saved from having to answer when Faith's husband, Chase, came over with Faith's daughter and son in tow.

Chase smiled at Ella and she tried to ignore the awk-

wardness as she greeted him. This was all she wanted.
A nice man who didn't make her nervous. Was that too
much to ask?

"Mom, can we go?" Louisa said. "I still have math
homework to finish."

"We're probably the only parents here whose kids are
begging to leave so they can get back to homework,"
Chase said with a grin.

"Thanks again for the great show, Ella," Faith said.
"We'll see you tomorrow. Now that we've been warned
the McKinley twins are coming, we'll make sure you
have reinforcements at practice tomorrow."

She could handle the twins. Their father was another
story.

As much as he enjoyed hanging out with other ranchers, shooting the, er, shinola, as his dad used to call it,
Beck decided it was time to head out. It was past the
boys' bedtime and their bus would be coming early.

"Gentlemen, it's been a pleasure but I need to call it
a night," he said.

There were more than a few good-hearted groans of
disappointment.

He loved the supportive ranching community here
in Pine Gulch. Friends and neighbors came through for
each other in times of need. He couldn't count the number of guys who had stepped in to help him after his
father died. When Stephanie left, he had needed help
again until he could find a good nanny and more than
one neighbor had come over without being asked to lend
a hand on the ranch.

The Broken Arrow would have gone under without
their aid and he knew he could never repay them. The

only thing he could do now was help out himself where he could.

As Beck waved goodbye and headed away from the group, he saw Curt Baker climb to his feet with the aid of his cane and follow after him. Beck slowed his steps so the older man could catch up.

"Thanks again for stepping in today and helping Manny unload the feed shipment."

"Glad I could help," he answered.

It was true. He admired Curt and owed the man. After Beckett's father died, Curt had been the first neighbor to step in and help him figure out what he was doing on the ranch. Now the tables were turned. Curt's Parkinson's disease limited his ability to care for his own holdings. He had reduced his herd significantly and brought in more help, but still struggled to take care of the day-to-day tasks involved in running a cattle ranch.

He had actually talked Curt into running with him to be copresidents of the local cattle growers association. It wasn't a tough job and gave Curt something else to focus on besides his health issues.

"Have you thought more on what we talked about over lunch?"

As if he could think about anything else. As much as he enjoyed cowboy folk songs, he'd had a hard time focusing on anything but Curt's stunning proposal that afternoon.

"You love the Baker's Dozen," he said. "There's no rush to sell it now, is there?"

Curt was quiet. "I'm not getting better. We both know that. There's only one direction this damn disease will go and that's south."

Parkinson's really sucked.

"I'm not in a hurry to sell. So far Manny and the other ranch hands are keeping things going—with help from you and Jax, of course—but you and I both know it's only a matter of time before I'll have to sell. I want to make sure I have things lined up ahead of time. Just wanted to plant the seed."

That little seed had certainly taken root. Hell, it was spreading like snakeweed.

The Broken Arrow was doing better than Beck ever dreamed, especially since he and his brother, Jax, had shifted so many of their resources to breeding exceptional cattle horses. They still ran about 500 cow-calf pair, but right now half the ranch's revenue was coming from the equine side of the business.

He would love the chance to expand his operation into the Baker's Dozen acreage, which had prime water rights along with it. He wasn't trying to build an empire here, but he had two boys to consider, as well as Jax. Though his brother seemed happy to play the field, someday that might change and he might want to settle down and become a family man.

Beck needed to make sure the Broken Arrow could support him, if that time came. It made perfect sense to grow his own operation into the adjacent property. It would be a big financial reach, but after several record-breaking years, he had the reserves to handle it.

"How does Ella feel about this?" he asked.

Curt shrugged. "What's not to like? You take over the work and we have money in the bank. She'll be fine. She could go back to Boston and not have to worry about me."

He wasn't sure he agreed with Curt's assessment of the Ella factor. Yeah, she didn't know anything about ranching and had only lived here with her father for a little longer than a year, but Ella was stubborn. She adored her father and had moved here to help him, though Curt seemed reluctant to lean on her too much.

"Anyway, we can worry about that later," Curt said. "My priority is to make sure I sell the land to someone who's actually going to ranch it, not turn it into condominiums. I've seen what you've done with the Broken Arrow since your father died and I have no doubt you'd give the same care to the Baker's Dozen."

"I appreciate that."

"No need to decide anything right now. We have plenty of time."

"You've given me a lot to chew on."

"That was my intent," Curt said. "Still need me to talk to Ella about taking your boys to the music thingy tomorrow?"

He winced, embarrassed that he'd even brought it up earlier. He was a grown man. He could talk to her himself, even if the woman did make him feel like he'd just been kicked by a horse, breathless and stupid and slow.

"I'll do it," he said. "I actually have a few things in town so should be able to take them tomorrow. When I get the chance, I'll try to talk to her then about future rehearsals."

He wasn't sure why his boys were so set on being in this Christmas program, but they were funny kids, with their own independent minds. He had always had the philosophy that he would try to support them in anything they tried. Basketball, soccer, after-school science clubs. Whatever.

Even when it meant he had to talk to Ella Baker.

Chapter Three

"Trevor. Colter. That's the last time I'm going to ask you. Please stop making silly noises. If you keep interrupting, we won't make it through all the songs we need to practice."

The twins gave Ella matching guilty looks. "Sorry, Miss Baker," Colter said.

"We'll be good. We promise," his brother added.

Somehow she was having a hard time believing that, especially given their track record in general and this practice in particular. After a full day of school, they were having a tough time sitting still and staying focused for the rehearsals, as she had fully expected.

She felt totally inadequate to deal with them on a December afternoon when they wanted to be running around outside, throwing snowballs and building snow forts.

Would it distract everyone too much if she had them

stand up and do jumping jacks for a minute? She decided it was worth a try. Sometimes a little burst of energy could do wonders for focus.

"Okay, speed workout. Everyone. How many elf jumping jacks can you do in one minute? Count to yourself. Go."

She timed them on her phone and by the end the children were all laughing and trying to outdo each other.

"Excellent. Okay, now close your eyes and we'll do one more moment of deep breathing. That's it. Perfect."

That seemed to refocus everyone and they made it through nearly every number without further incident, until the last one, "Away in a Manger."

The song sounded lovely, with all the children singing in tune and even enunciating the words—until the last line of the third verse, when Trevor started making noises like a certain explosive bodily function, which made the entire back row dissolve into laughter.

By the time they finished the ninety-minute rehearsal, though, she felt as wrung out as a dirty mitten left in the snow.

As soon as parents started arriving for their children, Hope popped in from the office of The Christmas Ranch with a mug of hot chocolate, which she thrust out to Ella.

"Here you go. Extra snowflake marshmallows. You deserve it. You survived the first rehearsal. It's all uphill from here."

"I hope so," she muttered. "Today was a bit of a disaster."

"I saw Beck's boys giving you a rough time," Hope said, her voice sympathetic.

"You could say that. It must be tough on them, coming straight from school to here."

Eight rehearsals. That's all they had. She could handle that, couldn't she?

"Do you need me to find more people to help you?"

She considered, then shook her head. "I think we should be okay with the two teenagers who volunteered. Everyone is so busy this time of year. I hate to add one more thing to someone else's plate."

"Because your schedule is so free and easy over the next few weeks, right?"

Hope had a point. Between the Christmas show, the care center where she volunteered and the two schools where she worked, Ella had concerts or rehearsals every single day between now and Christmas.

"At least I'm not a bestselling illustrator who also happens to be in charge of the number-one holiday attraction for hundreds of miles around."

"Lucky you," Hope said with a grin. "Want to trade?"

"Not a chance."

Hope wouldn't trade her life, either, Ella knew. She loved creating the Sparkle the Reindeer books, which had become a worldwide sensation over the last few years. She also adored running the ranch with her husband, Rafe, and raising their beautiful son.

"Let me know if you change your mind about needing more help," Hope said.

"I will."

After Hope headed away, Ella started cleaning up the mess of paper wrappers and leftover sheet music the children had left behind. She was gathering up her own things when a couple of boys trotted out of the gift shop.

Colter and Trevor. Was she supposed to be giving them a ride? Beck hadn't called her. He hadn't said a word to her about it. Had he just assumed she would do it without being asked?

That didn't really seem like something Beck would do. More likely, there was a miscommunication.

"Do you need me to call your dad to let him know we're done with rehearsal?"

Colter gave an exasperated sigh. "We told him and told him about it last night and this morning at breakfast. We took a note to school so we could ride a different bus here, then our dad was supposed to come get us when practice was done. I don't know where he is."

"Maybe we'll have to sleep here tonight," Trevor said. "I call under the Christmas tree!"

"You're not sleeping here tonight. I can give you a ride, but I need to talk to your dad first to make sure he's not on his way and just running late. I wouldn't want us to cross paths."

At least he hadn't just assumed she could take care of it. Slightly mollified, she pulled her phone out of her pocket. "Do you know his number?"

The boys each recited a different number, argued for a few moments, then appeared to come to a consensus.

She punched in the numbers they gave her without much confidence she would actually be connected to Beck, but to her surprise he answered.

"Broken Arrow," he said, with a brusqueness she should have expected, especially considering he probably didn't recognize her phone number.

Those two simple words in his deep, sexy voice seemed to shiver down her spine as if he'd trailed a finger down it.

"Beckett, this is Ella Baker. I was wondering…that

is, your sons were wondering, uh, are you coming to pick them up?"

Darn it, she *hated* being so tongue-tied around the man. She had all the poise and grace of a lumbering steer.

There was a long, awkward pause, then he swore. He quickly amended it. "Uh, shoot. I totally forgot about that. What time is rehearsal done?"

"About twenty minutes ago," she answered, letting a bit of tartness creep into her voice.

He sighed. "I've got the vet here looking at a sick horse. We're going to be another ten minutes or so, then I'll have to clean up a bit. Can you give me a half hour?"

He still couldn't seem to bring himself to ask for her help. Stubborn man. She glanced over at the boys, who were admiring the giant Christmas tree in the lodge. She wasn't sure she had the physical or mental capacity to keep them entertained and out of trouble for another half hour.

"I can give them a ride home, if you would like. It's an easy stop on my way back to the Baker's Dozen."

"Could you? That would be a big help. Thank you." The relief in his voice was palpable.

"You're welcome. Do you want me to drop them at the barn or the house?"

"The horse barn, if you don't mind. That's where I'm working."

She was suddenly having second thoughts, not sure she was ready to see him two days in a row.

"All right. We'll see you shortly, then."

"Thank you," he said again.

She managed to round up the boys in the nick of time, seconds before they were about to test how strong the garland over the mantel was by taking turns dangling from it.

How had Beck's house not burned down to the ground by now, with these two mischievous boys around?

"Why are you driving us home?" Colter asked when they had their seat belts on in her back seat. "Where's our dad?"

"He's taking care of a sick horse, he said. The vet's there with him and they lost track of time."

"That's Frisco. He was our mom's horse, but he's probably gonna die soon."

She wasn't sure how to reply to that, especially when he spoke in a matter-of-fact way. "I'm sorry."

"He's really old and too ornery for us to ride. He bites. Dad says he better not catch us near him," Trevor said.

She shivered, then hoped they couldn't see. She had to get over her fear of horses, darn it. After more than a year in horse and cattle country, she thought she would be past it—but then, twenty years hadn't made a difference, so why should the past year enact some miraculous change?

"You better do what he says."

"We don't want to ride that grumpy thing, anyway," Trevor said. "Why would we? We both have our own horses. Mine is named Oreo and Colt's is named Blackjack."

"Do you have a horse, Miss Baker?"

She remembered a sweet little roan mare she had adored more than anything in the world.

"I used to, when I was your age. Her name was Ruby. But I haven't been on a horse in a long, long time. We don't have any horses on the Baker's Dozen."

In one bold sweep, her dad had gotten rid of them all

twenty years ago, even though he had loved to ride, too. Thinking about it always made her sad.

"You could come ride our horses. We have like a million of them."

Familiar fear sidled up to her and said hello. "That's nice of you, Colter, but I don't know how to ride anymore. It's been a very long time since I've been in a saddle."

"We could teach you again," Trevor offered, with a sweet willingness that touched something deep inside. "I bet you'd pick it up again easy."

For a moment, she was very tempted by the offer but she would have to get past her phobia first. "That's very kind of you," she said, and left it at that. The boys didn't need to know about her issues.

"Hey, you know how to sing, right?" Colter said suddenly, changing the subject.

Considering she had one degree in music therapy and another in music education, she hoped so. "Yes. That is certainly something I do know how to do."

"And you play the guitar. You do it in school sometimes."

And the piano, violin and most other stringed instruments. "That's right."

"Could you teach us how to play a song?" Colter asked.

"And how to sing it, too?" Trevor said.

She glanced in her rearview mirror at their faces, earnestly eager. "Does either of you know how to play the guitar?"

"We both do, kind of," Colter said. "Uncle Dan taught us a couple chords last summer but then he said he wouldn't teach us anymore because we played too hard and broke all the strings on his guitar."

"Oh, dear."

These boys didn't do anything half-heartedly. She secretly hoped they would continue to be all-in as they grew up—with a little self-restraint when it was necessary, anyway.

"But we would never do that to your guitar, if you let us practice on it," he assured her with a grave solemnity that almost made her smile.

"We promise," his twin said. "We would be super careful."

She couldn't believe she would even entertain the idea for a moment, but she couldn't deny she was curious about the request. "What song are you trying to learn how to play and sing?"

"It's a good one. 'Christmas for the Cowboy.' Have you heard that one?"

"I'm not sure."

"It's about this cowboy and he has to work on Christmas Eve and ride his horse in the snow and stuff," Trevor informed her.

"He's real mad about it, and thinks it's not fair and he wants to be inside where it's warm, then the animals help him remember that Christmas is about peace on earth and stuff."

"And baby Jesus and wise men and shepherds," Trevor added.

"That sounds like a good one."

She combed through her memory bank but wasn't sure if she had ever heard it.

"It's our dad's favorite Christmas song in the whole wide world. He hums it all the time and keeps the CD in his pickup truck."

"Do you know who sings it?" she asked. It would be

much easier to track down the guitar chords if she could at least have that much info.

The boys named a country music group whose name she recognized. She wasn't very familiar with their body of work.

"So can you teach us?" Colter asked as they neared the turnoff for the Broken Arrow. "It has to be with the guitar, too."

"Please?" Trevor asked. "Pretty please with Skittles on top?"

Well, she did like Skittles. She hid a smile. "Why is this so important to you? Why do you want to learn the song so badly?"

As she glanced in the rearview mirror, she saw the boys exchange looks. She had noticed before they did that quite often, as if passing along some nonverbal, invisible, twin communication that only they understood.

"It's for our dad," Trevor finally said. "He works hard all the time and takes care of us and stuff and we never have a good present to give him at Christmas."

"Except things we make in school, and that's usually just dumb crap," Colter said. "Pictures and clay bowls and stuff."

Ella had a feeling the art teacher she shared a classroom with probably wouldn't appreciate that particularly blunt assessment.

"When we went to bed last night after the concert, we decided we should learn that song and play it for our dad because he loves it so much, but we don't know the right words. We always sing it wrong."

"Hey, maybe after we learn it, we could play and sing it in the Christmas program," Colter said.

"Yeah," Trevor said, "Like that guy and his wranglers last night."

She didn't know how to respond, afraid to give the boys false hope. She didn't even know what song they were talking about, let alone whether it was appropriate for a Christmas program designed for senior citizens.

"I'm afraid I'm not familiar with that song—" she began.

"You could learn it, couldn't you?" Colter said.

"It's probably not even too hard."

As she turned into the ranch, they passed a large pasture containing about a dozen horses. Two of them cantered over to the fence line, then raced along beside her SUV, their manes and tails flying out behind them.

She felt the familiar panic, but something else, a long-buried regret for what she had lost.

"If I can find the song and agree to teach you, I need something from the two of you in return."

"Let me guess. You want us to quit messing around at rehearsal." Colter said this in the same resigned tone someone might use after being told they faced an IRS audit.

"Absolutely. That's one of my conditions. You told me you could behave, but today wasn't a very good example of that. I need to be able to trust you to keep your word."

"Sorry, Miss Baker."

"We'll do better, we promise."

How many times had the boys uttered those very same words to one voice of authority or other? No doubt they always meant it, but something told her they would follow through this time. It touched her heart that they wanted to give this gift to their father, who had sacri-

ficed and struggled and refused to give up custody after
their mother died.

She wanted to help them give something back to
him—and she wanted something in return, something
that made her palms suddenly feel sweaty on the steering wheel.

"That is one of my conditions. And I'm very firm
about it."

She paused, sucked in a breath, then let it out in a rush
and spoke quickly before she could change her mind.

"I also have one more condition."

"What?" Trevor asked.

Her heart was pounding so hard, she could barely hear
herself think. This was foolish. Why did she think two
seven-year-old boys could help her overcome something
she had struggled with for twenty years?

"You said you could teach me how to ride horses
again. I would like that, very much. I told you it's been
a long time since I've been on a horse. I…miss it."

More than she had even dared acknowledge to herself.

Once, horses had been her passion. She had dreamed
about them, talked about them, drew pictures of them,
even during the months when she was living in Boston
during the ten months out of the year her mother had
custody of her. It used to drive Elizabeth crazy.

Everything had changed when she was eight.

"You really can't ride?" Trevor said. "You said that before but I didn't think you meant it. You're a grown-up."

These boys probably spent more time in the saddle
than out of it. She had seen them before as she was driving by the ranch, racing across the field and looking utterly carefree. Until now, Ella hadn't realized how very
much she had envied them.

"Not everyone is as lucky as you two," she said as she pulled up to the large red indoor horse barn and arena. "I learned how to ride when I was a child, but then I had a bad fall and it's been…hard for me ever since."

Hard was an understatement. What she didn't tell the boys was that she had a completely reasonable terror of horses.

She had been only a year older than the boys, on a visit here with her father. Her sweet little Ruby had been nursing an injury so she had insisted to her father she could handle one of the other geldings on a ride with him along their favorite trail. The horse had been jittery, though, and had ended up being spooked by a snake on the trail just as they were crossing a rocky slope.

Not only had she fallen from the horse, but she had also tumbled thirty feet down the mountainside.

After being airlifted to Idaho Falls, she had ended up in a medically induced coma, with a head injury, several broken vertebrae and a crushed leg. She had spent months in the hospital and rehab clinics. Even after extensive therapy, she still limped when she was tired.

Her injuries had marked the final death knell to the marriage her parents had tried for years to patch back together. They had been separated on and off most of her childhood before then. After her riding accident, her mother completely refused to send her to the ranch.

The custody battle had been epic. In the process, a great gulf had widened between her and her father, one that she was still trying to bridge, twenty years later.

If she could only learn to ride, conquer her fear, perhaps Curt Baker wouldn't continue to see her as a fragile doll who needed to be protected at all costs.

"I know the basics," she told the boys now. "I just need

some pointers. It's a fair trade, don't you think? I teach you a few chords on the guitar and you let me practice riding horses."

The boys exchanged looks, their foreheads furrowed as they considered her request. She caught some furtive whispers but couldn't hear what they said.

While she waited for them to decide, Ella wondered if she was crazy. She couldn't believe she was actually considering this. What could these boys teach her, really? She was about to tell them she had changed her mind about the riding lessons but would still teach them the song when Trevor spoke for both of them.

"Sure. We could do that. When do you want to practice? How about Saturday?"

"We can't!" Trevor said to his brother. "We have practice Saturday, remember?"

"Oh, yeah. But maybe in the afternoon, when we're done."

Why was she even considering throwing one more thing into her packed schedule? She couldn't do it. Ella wiped her sweaty palms on her skirt. "We can forget this. It was a silly idea."

"Why?" Trevor asked, his features confused. "We want you to teach us how to play and sing a song for our dad's Christmas present and you want to learn how to ride a horse better so you don't fall off. We can teach each other."

"It will be fun. You'll see. And maybe you could even buy one of our dad's horses after you learn how to ride again."

That was pushing things. Maybe she first ought to see if she could spend five minutes around horses without having a panic attack.

"So can you come Saturday afternoon?" Trevor asked.

"Our dad won't be home, so that would be good. Then he won't need to know why we're teaching you how to ride horses. Because otherwise, we'd have to tell him it's a trade. That would ruin the surprise."

"I...think I can come Saturday." Oh, she was crazy.

"Yay! This will be fun. You'll see."

She wasn't so sure. Before she could come up with an answer, the door to the barn opened and Beck came striding out with that loose-limbed, sexy walk she always tried—and failed—to ignore.

He had someone else with him. Ben Caldwell, she realized, the veterinarian in town whose wife, Caidy, had a magical singing voice. She barely noticed the other man, too busy trying not to stare at Beckett.

Her hands felt clammy again as she opened her car door, but this time she knew it wasn't horses making her nervous.

Chapter Four

"You know, it might be time to say goodbye."

Ben Caldwell spoke gently as he ran a calming hand down Frisco's neck. "He's tired, he's cranky, he can't see and he's half-lame. I can keep coming out here and you can keep on paying me, but eventually I'm going to run out of things I can do to help him feel better."

Beckett was aware of a familiar ache in his gut. He knew it would be soon but didn't like to think about it. "I know. Not yet, though."

The vet nodded his understanding but that didn't make Beck feel any less stupid. No doubt Dr. Caldwell wondered why he had such a soft spot for this horse that nobody had been able to ride for five years. Frisco had always been bad-tempered and high-spirited, but somehow Stephanie had loved him, anyway. Beck wasn't quite ready to say goodbye yet.

He shook the vet's hand. "Thanks, Ben. I appreciate you coming by."

"You got it."

Sal, one of Beck's border collies, waddled over to them, panting a welcome. The veterinarian scratched her under the chin and gently patted her side.

"She hasn't had those pups yet."

"Any day now. We're on puppy watch."

"You'll call me if she has any troubles, right?"

"You know it."

He had great respect for Ben. Though Beck hadn't been too sure about the city vet when the man moved to town a handful of years ago, Dr. Caldwell had proved himself over and over. He'd also married a friend of his, Caidy Bowman, who had gone to school with Beck.

They were finishing up with Frisco when he heard a vehicle pull up outside. Beck's heartbeat accelerated, much to his chagrin.

"You expecting somebody?" Ben asked.

"That would be Ella Baker. I, uh, forgot to pick the boys up from rehearsal at The Christmas Ranch and she was nice enough to bring them home for me."

"That Christmas program is all the buzz at my place, too," Ben said. "My kids can't wait."

Ben had been a widower with two children, a boy and a girl, when he moved to town. Beck sometimes had Ben's daughter babysit the twins in a pinch.

The two men walked outside and Beck was again aware of his pulse in his ears. This was so stupid, that he couldn't manage to stop staring at Ella as she climbed out of her SUV.

Ben sent him a sidelong look and Beck really hoped the man didn't notice his ridiculous reaction.

"I'll get out of your way," Ben said. "Think about what I said."

"I will. Thanks again."

Ella and the boys both waved at the veterinarian as they climbed out of her vehicle.

"Hey, Dad! Hey!" His boys rushed over to him, arms wide, and he hugged them, wondering if there would ever come a time in his life when they didn't feel like the best damn thing that had ever happened to him.

He doubted it. He couldn't even imagine how much poorer his life would be without Trevor and Colter. Whenever he was tempted to regret his ill-conceived marriage, he only had to hug his boys and remember that all the rest of the mess and ugliness had been worth it.

"Hey, guys. How was practice? Did you behave yourselves?"

"Um, sure," Colter said.

"Kind of," his brother hedged.

Which meant not at all. He winced.

"We're gonna do better," Colter assured him. "We promised Miss Baker. Me and Trevor thought maybe we could run around the building three times before we go inside to practice, to get our energy out."

"That sounds like a plan."

It was a strategy he sometimes employed when they struggled to focus on homework at night, taking them on a good walk around the ranch so they could focus better.

"I'm starving," Trevor said. "Can I have a cheese stick?"

"Me, too!" Colter said.

"Yeah. You know where they are."

The boys ran into the barn, heading for the fridge inside the office, where he kept a few snacks.

He turned to her. Like his father always said, better to eat crow when it was fresh. It tasted better hot and was much easier to swallow.

"How big of an apology do I owe you for the boys' behavior?"

To his surprise, she smiled, something she didn't do around him very often. For some reason, the woman didn't seem to like him very much.

"On a scale of one to ten?" she asked. "Probably a seven."

"I'm going to take that as a win."

Her smile widened. It made her whole face glow. With a few snowflakes falling in her hair and the slanted afternoon sun hitting her just right, the universe seemed to be making it impossible for him to look away.

"It's hard for two seven-year-old boys to be in school all day, then take a long bus ride, then have to sit and behave for another hour and a half," she said. "I understand that. They have energy to burn and need somewhere to put it. Today was hard because there was a lot of sitting around while we practiced songs. Things won't be as crazy for our next practice, I'm sure."

"It really does help if they can work out a little energy."

"We did elf jumping jacks. You're right, things were better after that."

She paused, her smile sliding away. He had the feeling she was uncomfortable about something. Or maybe he was the only uncomfortable one here.

"Do you need me to give the boys a ride to the rest of our practices?" she finally asked. "I can take them with me to The Christmas Ranch after school and bring them back here when practice is over."

Her generous offer startled him. The night before, he had wanted to ask her the same thing, but in the light of day, the request had seemed entirely too presumptuous.

"Are you sure that wouldn't be a problem?"

"You're right next door. It's only five minutes out of my way, to bring them up here to the house. I don't mind, really."

"That's very gracious of you. If you're sure it won't be an inconvenience, I would appreciate it."

"I don't mind. I should warn you, they might be a little later coming home than some of the other children, since I have to straighten up our rehearsal space after we're done. Perhaps they can help me put away chairs after practice."

"Absolutely. They're good boys and will work hard, as long as they have a little direction."

The wind was kicking up, blowing down out of the foothills with that peculiar smell of an approaching storm. She shivered a little and he felt bad for keeping her standing out here. He could have invited her inside the horse barn, at least.

"I really do appreciate it," he said, feeling as big and rough and awkward as he always did around her soft, graceful beauty. "To be honest, I wasn't sure how I would juggle everything this week. I'm supposed to be going out of town tomorrow until Monday to look at a couple of horses and I hate complicating the boys' schedule more than I have to for Uncle Dan and Jax."

"No problem."

"Thanks. I owe you one."

"You do," she answered firmly. "And here's how you can pay me back. We're signing up drivers for the night of the show to pick up some of the senior citizens who don't like driving in the snow. Add your name to the list and we can be even."

That would be no hardship for him. It would take up one evening of his life and he could fit a half-dozen senior citizens in his crew cab pickup.

"Sure. I can do that."

"Okay. Deal."

To his surprise, she thrust out her hand to seal the agreement, as if they were bartering cattle or signing a treaty. After a beat, he took it. Her fingers were cool, small, smooth, and he didn't want to let go. He was stunned by his urge to tug her against him and kiss that soft, sweet mouth.

He came to his senses just an instant before he might have acted on the impulse and released her fingers. He saw confusion cloud her gaze but something else, too. A little spark of awareness he instantly recognized.

"I need to, that is, I have to…my dad will be waiting for me."

"Give my best regards to Curt," he said.

The words were a mistake. He knew it as soon as he spoke them. Her mouth tightened and that little glimmer of awareness disappeared, crowded out by something that looked like resentment.

"I'll do that, though I'm sure he already knows he has your best regards," she said stiffly. "The feeling is mutual, I'm sure."

He frowned, again feeling awkward and not sure what he should say. Yes, he and her father got along well. He respected Curt, enjoyed the man's company, and was grateful he was in a position to help him. Why did that bother her?

Did she know Curt had offered to sell him the ranch?

He was hesitant to ask, for reasons he couldn't have defined.

"I should go. It's been a long day. I'll bring the boys back from practice tomorrow and take care of Saturday, too."

"Sounds good. I won't be here, but Jax and Dan will be."

She nodded and climbed into her SUV in her fancy leather boots and slim skirt.

He watched her drive away for much longer than he should have, wondering why he felt so awkward around her. Everyone in town seemed to like Ella. Though she had moved back only a year ago, she had somehow managed to fuse herself into the fabric of this small Idaho community.

He liked her, too. That was a big part of the problem. He couldn't be around her without wondering if her skin was as soft as it looked, her hair as silky, her mouth as delicious.

He had to get over this stupid attraction, but he had no idea how.

He was so busy watching after her taillights, he didn't notice the boys had come out until Trevor spoke.

"Hey, Dad. What are you lookin' at?" his son asked.

"Is it a wolf?" Colter vibrated with excitement at the idea. They had driven up to Yellowstone for the weekend a month ago and had seen four of them loping along the Lamar Valley road. Since then, the boys had been fascinated with the idea of wolves, especially after Beck explained the Pine Gulch area was part of the larger far-ranging territory of the various Yellowstone packs.

"Nope. No wolves," he said now. "I'm just enjoying the sight of our pretty ranch."

His sons stood beside him, gazing at the ranch along with him.

This was what should matter to him, passing on a legacy for these boys. He had worked his ass off to bring the Broken Arrow ranch back from the brink since his father died a decade ago. The ranch was thriving now, producing fine cattle and the best quarter-horse stock in the entire region.

He intended to do his best to protect that legacy for his boys and for his younger brother, so he could have something more than bills and barren acreage to give them after he was gone.

He would build on it, too, when he had the chance. Any smart man would take any opportunity to expand his holdings. Beck couldn't let anything stand in the way, especially not a pretty city girl who wore completely impractical boots and made him think things he knew he shouldn't.

Ella's pulse was still racing uncomfortably as she drove the short distance between his ranch and the Baker's Dozen.

Why, oh, why did Beck McKinley have to be so darned gorgeous? She didn't know how it was possible, but he seemed to get better looking every time she saw him.

This crush was becoming ridiculous. She felt like a giddy girl who had never talked to a man before. Completely untrue. She'd been engaged once, for heaven's sake, to a junior partner in her stepfather's law practice.

Okay, she had been engaged for a month. That counted, right?

On paper, Devin had been ideal. Handsome, earnest, ambitious. They enjoyed the same activities, listened to the same music, shared the same friends. She had known him since third grade and dated him all through college. Her mother and stepfather adored him and everyone said they made a perfect couple.

He proposed on her twenty-sixth birthday, with a ring that had been gorgeous and showy. Shortly afterward, they had started planning their wedding.

Well, her mother had started planning her wedding.

Ella's job in the process appeared to consist of leafing through bridal magazines and nodding her head when her mother made suggestion after suggestion about venues and catering companies and dress shops.

Three weeks into her engagement, she found out her father had Parkinson's. Not from Curt, of course. That would have been too straightforward. No, his longtime housekeeper, Alina, wife to his longtime foreman, Manny Guzman, called to let her know he had fallen again. That was a news flash to her, since she didn't know he had fallen before.

After some probing, she learned Curt had been diagnosed a year earlier and had kept it from her. Apparently he had balance issues and had fallen a few times before, requiring help from one of the hands to get back up.

This time, his fall had been more serious, resulting in a broken hip. She had taken leave from her job and immediately caught a flight to Idaho the next day, which hadn't made Devin very happy. After two weeks of him pleading with her to come back, she realized to her chagrin that she didn't want to go back—and worse, that she had barely given the man second thought.

She didn't love him. How could she possibly merge her life with someone she didn't love? It wasn't worth it, only to make her mother happy.

Ella had flown back to Boston, returned his ring and ended the engagement. He hadn't been heartbroken, which only seemed to reinforce her realization that theirs had been a relationship borne out of convenience and familiarity.

They would have been content together. She wanted to think so, anyway, but she wasn't sure they would have been truly happy.

Devin had never once made her insides feel as if a hundred butterflies were doing an Irish step dance. Not like…

She shied away from the thought. Yes, Beck was hot. Yes, she was attracted to him and he left her giddy and breathless.

So what?

She didn't *want* to be attracted to him. It was pathetic, really, especially when it was clear the man thought she was useless out here in ranching country.

Join the crowd, she wanted to tell him. He and her father ought to form a club.

Oh, wait. They already had formed a mutual admiration society that completely excluded her.

She sighed, frustrated all over again at her stubborn father, who couldn't see that she was capable of so much more than he believed.

A blue pickup truck was parked in front of the Baker's Dozen ranch house as Ella pulled up, and she made a face. She recognized the truck as belonging to Chris Soldado, the physical and occupational therapist who came to the house twice a month to work with her dad, both for his ongoing recovery from the broken hip and to help him retain as much use of his limbs as possible as his Parkinson's progressed.

He must be working after-hours. She grimaced at the prospect. His visits always left Curt sore and cranky. More sore and cranky than usual, anyway.

As she let herself in, she found Chris Soldado and her father in the great room. Her father was leaning heavily on his cane while Chris seemed to be putting equipment back into his bag. Chris was a great guy who had been coming a couple times a month for as long as she had been back in Pine Gulch. He was firm but compassionate with Curt and didn't let him get away with much.

"Hi, Chris," she said with a smile.

"Hey there, Ella," he said. He gave her a flirtatious smile in return. "I'm just on my way out. I was telling your dad, he needs to be doing these exercises on his own, every day. That's the best way to retain as much mobility as he can for as long as possible. Make sure of it, okay?"

She tried to nag, but it usually only ended up frustrating both of them. "I'll do that. Thanks."

"This will probably be my last visit for this year. I'll see you in January, Mr. Baker."

Her father made a face but nodded. He looked tired, his features lined with strain.

She let the therapist out, then returned back to her dad and kissed him on the cheek. He needed to shave, something she knew was difficult for him with the trembling of his hands. That was one more area where he didn't want her help.

Maybe she ought to ask Beck to help Curt shave, since he was so good at everything else.

She sighed. "How was your day?"

"I just had physical therapy and that was a high point."

Oh, she missed the kind, loving father of her childhood. Big, hale, hearty. Wonderful.

He was still wonderful, she reminded herself. She just had to work through the occasionally unpleasant bits to get there.

"How about yours?" he asked, which she appreciated. He didn't always think to ask. "You're late getting home, aren't you?"

"Yes. Remember, I told you I would be late for the next few weeks. We had our first practice for the Christmas pageant."

"Oh, right. It slipped my mind during the torture session. How did it go?"

"Good, for the most part. The McKinley twins caused a bit of trouble but nothing I couldn't handle."

"Those boys are rascals," Curt said, but she heard clear admiration in his voice. "Alina left shepherd's pie. She said we just had to bake it but after Chris showed up, I forgot to turn on the oven."

"I can do that. Let me help you to your chair."

"No. I'm fine. If I sit in that recliner, I'll just fall asleep like an old man. I'll come in the kitchen with you."

That was an unexpected gift, as well. She decided to savor the small victories as she led the way to the kitchen. She fussed until he sat on one of the kitchen chairs, then she poured him a glass of water before turning on the oven and pulling out the potato-topped casserole that had always been a favorite of her father.

"So tell me what those twins were up to today," he said. Curt always seemed to get a kick out of Beck's boys and their hijinks.

"Nothing too egregious."

While she made a salad and set the table, she told him

stories about the boys. He laughed heartily when she mentioned the bodily noises during "Away in a Manger" and about them trying to hang from the garland, and she was suddenly grateful beyond measure for those twins and their energy, and for providing this lighthearted moment she could share with the father she loved.

Chapter Five

"That was excellent. Really excellent," Ella said, praising the two little cowboys seated at a table in the classroom she shared with the part-time art teacher.

She had arranged for Trevor and Colter to stay after school for a half hour so they could rehearse the cowboy ballad they wanted to sing for their father. She would drive them out to The Christmas Ranch when they were finished.

This had been the most logical rehearsal spot, even if the walls were currently adorned with collage after collage of grinning Santas made out of dry macaroni and cotton-puff beards.

Fortunately, all those Santas checking to see whether they were naughty or nice didn't seem to bother Trevor and Colter McKinley.

"We sound good enough to be on the radio, huh?" Trevor said.

She envied their sheer confidence, even as it made her smile. "Definitely," she answered. "You picked up the words and melody of the chorus perfectly. Why don't we try the whole thing from the beginning? Straighten up in your seat, now. You'll sing your best if your lungs have room to expand and they can't do that when you're all hunched over."

The boys sat up straight and straightened their collars as if they were preparing to take the stage at the Vienna opera house. She smiled, completely charmed by them. If she wasn't careful, these two troublemakers would worm their way right into her heart.

"Okay. Hit it," Colter said.

"Please," his twin added conscientiously.

They had decided that because of time constraints, it would be better if she just accompanied them so they didn't have to learn the words to the song and the unfamiliar guitar chords at the same time. She played the music she had found, the first gentle notes of the Christmas song.

The boys sang the lines in unison, their voices clear and pure and quite lovely. Their voices blended perfectly. She could only imagine how good it would sound if they could learn a little harmony.

They could work on that. For now, she wanted to focus on making sure they knew the words and phrasing of the song.

"That sounded really great," she said, after they went through the song four more times in a row.

"Our dad's going to love it," Trevor declared.

"I'm sure you're right." She glanced at the clock. "We had better run or we'll be late for practice with the rest of the children. We can run through the song a few more times on the way."

They grabbed their coats and yanked on backpacks while she prepared to close up the classroom.

"We'll meet you by the office," Colter said. Before she could call them back, they headed out of the classroom. She locked the door and was about to follow after when the fifth-grade teacher from across the hall opened her own door.

"Was that really the McKinley twin terrors I heard in here?" Susan Black looked flabbergasted.

"Yes. They asked me to help them prepare a song they could perform as a gift to their father for Christmas."

The older woman shook her head. "How did you get them to sit still long enough to even learn a line? I think I may seriously have to think about retirement before those two hit fifth grade."

"They like to sing. Sometimes it's just a matter of finding the right switch."

"You've got the magic touch, I guess."

She had no idea why the boys were beginning to respond to her, she thought as she walked toward the office, but she wasn't about to jinx things by questioning it too much.

The boys were waiting impatiently for her and raced ahead when she opened the outside door. They found her SUV in the nearly empty parking lot immediately—no surprise, as she'd given them a ride just the day before.

"Thanks again for helping us," Trevor said when they were safely seat-belted in the back and she was on her way.

"It's my pleasure," she told them.

"Are you still coming tomorrow to ride horses?"

That panic shivered through her and she almost told them to forget about that part of the deal. Two things stopped her. They were proud little cowboys and she sensed they wouldn't appreciate being beholden to her for anything. And second, she knew she couldn't give in to her fear or it would control the rest of her life.

"Are you sure it's okay with your dad?" She couldn't quite keep the trepidation from her voice.

"He won't care and he's gonna be gone, anyway."

"Oh, right. He's looking at a couple of horses."

"Yep. We talked to our uncle Jax and he said he can help us saddle up the easiest horse on the ranch for you."

"That's Creampuff," Colter said. "She's a big softie."

"You'll like her," Trevor assured her. "Even though she likes to wander out when she gets the chance, Dad says he could put a kitten on her back and she'd never knock it off."

"Sounds perfect for me, then," Ella said, trying not to show her nervousness.

"Great. So just wear stuff you can ride in tomorrow. Boots and jeans. You know. Not teacher clothes."

Apparently they didn't approve of her favorite green wool sweater set and dressy dove-gray slacks.

"Got it. I'll see if I can find something a little more appropriate," she said.

"It will be fun. You'll see," Colter said.

She had serious reservations, but tried to swallow them down as they arrived at The Christmas Ranch for rehearsal.

First things first. She had to make it through two more practices before she could have time to worry about her upcoming horseback-riding lesson.

"We were good today, don't you think?"

After rehearsal on Saturday, Ella glanced in the rear-view mirror at the two boys sitting in her back seat.

"You really were." She had to hope they didn't hear the note of wonder in her voice. "And yesterday, too. You paid attention, you stayed in your seats, you didn't distract your neighbors. Good job, guys."

"Told you we could be. It wasn't even that hard. We just had to pretend we were dead mice."

"Dead mice who could still sing," Trevor added.

Ella tried to hide her smile. "Whatever you did, it worked perfectly. Let's see if we can do it again next week, through the rest of the rehearsals we have left until the show."

"We will be," Trevor said. "We promised you, and our dad says a man's word is his wand."

It took her a second to fit the pieces together. "I think he probably said bond. That means a commitment."

"Oh, yeah. That was it. A man's word is his bond."

That sounded like something Beckett McKinley would say to his sons.

He was a good father. The boys were high-strung, but their hearts were in the right place. They were working hard to prepare a Christmas gift for their father and that day she had also watched them show great kindness to Taft Bowman's stepdaughter, who had Down syndrome and some developmental delays. She was older than they were by a few years but they still seemed to have appointed themselves her champion.

She should tell Beckett what good young men he was raising. Something told her he didn't hear that very often.

She pushed away thoughts of the man, grateful at least that she wouldn't have to see him today. She was stressed enough about riding the horses. She didn't need to add any additional anxiety into the mix.

As she drove up the snow-packed road to the ranch

house, those same horses that had greeted them the first time she brought the boys home raced alongside her SUV, a beautiful but terrifying sight in the afternoon sunlight.

She wouldn't be riding one of those energetic creatures. She would be riding a horse named Creampuff. How scary could something named Creampuff really be?

Terrifying enough that she felt as if her heart was going to pound out of her chest. She let out a breath. Why was she putting herself through this, again? It wouldn't make any difference with Curt. Her father loved her but he couldn't see her as anything but fragile, delicate, someone to be protected at all costs.

She pushed away the thought. This wasn't for her father. She needed to ride again for *herself*. She needed to prove to herself she could do it, that she could overcome her fears and finally tackle this anxiety. The opportunity had presented itself through these twins and she couldn't afford to miss it.

"Where should I park?" she asked as she approached the buildings clustered around the ranch house. "Where do you think we will be having this lesson?"

"Uncle Jax said we could use the riding barn. He said he would have Creampuff all ready for you. But then Uncle Dan made us promise we'd stop at the house first to grab some lunch and put on our boots."

"That sounds like a good idea. I need to change my clothes, anyway."

Despite the boys' fashion advice, Ella had worn a skirt and sweater to the Saturday rehearsal, as if preparing for a day at school. It seemed silly in retrospect, but she hadn't wanted to appear in jeans. In her experience, she tended to command more respect with her students when she was a little dressed up.

Her riding clothes were packed into a small bag on the passenger seat beside her, but she hadn't given much practical thought to when and where she would actually change into them. She should have had the foresight to do it at The Christmas Ranch before they left.

They directed her where to park and she pulled her SUV into a driveway in back of the house. The boys led the way inside, straight to the kitchen.

They found Daniel McKinley, Beck's uncle, wearing an apron and loading dishes into the dishwasher.

"There you two are. Howdy, Miss Baker."

She smiled at him. As always, she was delighted by his old-fashioned, courteous nature and ready smile.

He was quite a charmer in his day, she had heard— a bachelor cowboy who cut a broad swath through the female population of the county. Now he was over seventy with a bad back and struggled almost as much as her father to get around these days.

"You ready for your riding lesson?" Dan asked, offering her a smile that still held plenty of charm.

Would she ever be? "Yes," she lied. "I can't wait."

"These boys will get you up on a horse, you wait and see. Best little cowboys I ever did see. They'll have you barrel racing in the rodeo by summer."

That was far beyond what she even wanted to attempt. She could only pray she would be able to stay in the saddle.

"I'm makin' sandwiches, if you want one," he offered. "Nothing grand, just grilled ham and cheese. It's one of the four things I know how to cook."

"What are the other three?" she asked, genuinely curious.

"Coffee, hot dogs and quesadillas. As long as I'm only

making them with cheese and salsa. Oh, I can do scrambled eggs, too, if you've got a hankering."

She had to smile, completely enchanted by him. "I'm great with a ham sandwich. Thanks so much for offering."

"It's no trouble. Just as easy to make four sandwiches as it is three, I suspect."

"I appreciate it, anyway. May I help you?"

"You can help me by sitting down and relaxing. Something tells me you don't do enough of that, Miz Baker."

True enough, especially the last month. She would have time to rest after the holidays.

"If it's all right with you, I would like to find somewhere to change into more appropriate clothing for a riding lesson."

"You can use Beck's bedroom. First door on the right."

She instantly wanted to protest. Was there really nowhere else in this big, beautiful log house for her to change, besides Beckett McKinley's bedroom? She didn't want to know where he slept, where he dressed, where he probably walked around in his briefs.

She let out a breath, aware that she would sound completely ridiculous if she raised a single irrational objection to his suggestion.

Nothing left but to accept with grace, she decided. "That sounds good. I'll change my clothes and then come help you with lunch."

He pointed her on her way, his leathery features split into a smile. Unlike her father, Dan McKinley still appeared to have a healthy appetite. He limped around the kitchen but other than that, his skin was firm and pink instead of the sallow tones her father sometimes had.

Curt had probably lost twenty pounds in the months

she had been back in Pine Gulch. He was still large-framed, but his clothing all sat loosely on him these days and he wore suspenders to keep up his pants.

It made her sad to see the comparison between the two men, though she reminded herself she couldn't change the course of her father's disease. She could only try to make his world as comfortable and accessible as possible.

She gripped her tote bag and hurried down the hall lined with beautiful western artwork, highlighted by tasteful inset lighting.

As she might have expected, judging by the rest of the house, Beck's bedroom was gorgeous, spacious and comfortable, with a river-rock fireplace in one corner and expansive windows that looked over both his ranch and her father's. It was dominated by a massive log bed, neatly made, with a masculine comforter in tones of dark blue and green.

The room smelled of him, of sagebrush and leather and rainy summer afternoons in the mountains.

She inhaled deeply and felt something visceral and raw spring to life inside her. Oh. She wanted to stand right here and just savor it.

That bed. Her imagination suddenly seemed entirely too vivid. A snowy night and the two of them tangled together under that soft blanket, with all those hard muscles hers alone to explore.

"Snap out of it," she ordered herself, just seconds before she would have pulled his pillow up to her face to inhale.

Good grief. She didn't come here to moon over Beck. She was here to conquer her fears and tackle something that terrified her.

Okay, he terrified her, too. But this was about horseback riding.

With renewed determination, she quickly kicked off her dressy boots and slipped down her skirt, then pulled on her favorite weathered jeans.

Her Christmas sweater with the reindeer and sleigh had been fun for the kids during rehearsal for the program, but would be too bulky and uncomfortable under her coat while she was riding.

She started to pull it over her head but the textured heavy yarn that was part of the design tangled in one of the combs she'd used to pull her hair back. Shoot. If she tugged it too hard, she would rip the sweater and ruin it. She didn't want that. It was one of her favorites, a gift from a friend in Boston.

With her hands above her head and the sweater covering her face, she tried to extricate the design from her hair comb when suddenly she heard the door open.

Panic burst through her and she almost crossed her arms over her chest. At the last minute, she remembered she still had on the plain white T-shirt she wore underneath the sweater.

"Who's there?" she demanded, her face buried in sweater.

"Beck McKinley," a deep voice drawled. "I believe I should be the one asking questions, Miss Baker. It's my bedroom, after all, and to be perfectly honest, I can't begin to guess what you might be doing in it."

She closed her eyes, wishing she could disappear. She should have known. Who else would it be? Wasn't that just the way her luck went? The one person she didn't want to see would, of course, be the one who stumbled in on an embarrassing moment.

She would have far preferred his brother, Jax, who flirted with everyone and could be handled simply by flirting right back.

She ought to just yank down the sweater and rip it, but she couldn't quite bring herself to do that.

"I'm sorry. Your uncle told me I could use your room to change into riding clothes. Didn't he tell you?"

"I haven't talked to Dan since breakfast. I've been holed up in my office on the other side of the house all morning. Riding clothes, Ella?"

She did *not* want to have this conversation with him with her sweater tangled around her head. The only bright spot in this entire miserable predicament was that she was wearing a T-shirt underneath the sweater. She couldn't imagine how mortifying if he had walked in on her in only her bra.

"It's a long story. I can tell you, but would you help me with my sweater first?"

After a pregnant pause, he finally spoke. "Uh, what seems to be the trouble?"

His voice had an odd, strangled note to it. Was he laughing at her? Where she couldn't see him, she couldn't be quite sure. "It's stuck in my hair comb. I don't want to rip the sweater—or yank out my hair, for that matter."

He was silent, then she felt the air stir as he moved closer. The scent of him was stronger now, masculine and outdoorsy, and everything inside her sighed a welcome.

He stood close enough that she could feel the heat radiating from him. She caught her breath, torn between a completely prurient desire for the moment to last at least a little longer and a wild hope that the humiliation of being caught in this position would be over quickly.

"Hold still," he said. Was his voice deeper than usual?

She couldn't quite tell. She did know it sent tiny delicious shivers down her spine.

"You've really done a job here," he said after a moment.

"I know. I'm not quite sure how it tangled so badly."

She would have to breathe soon or she was likely to pass out. She forced herself to inhale one breath and then another until she felt a little less light-headed.

"Almost there," he said, his big hands in her hair, then a moment later she felt a tug and the sweater slipped all the way over her head.

"There you go."

"Thank you." She wanted to disappear, to dive under that great big log bed and hide away. Instead, she forced her mouth into a casual smile. "These Christmas sweaters can be dangerous. Who knew?"

She was blushing. She could feel her face heat and wondered if he noticed. This certainly counted among the most embarrassing moments of her life.

"Want to explain again what you're doing in my bedroom, tangled up in your clothes?" he asked.

She frowned at his deliberately risqué interpretation of something that had been innocent. Mostly.

There *had* been that secret moment when she had closed her eyes and imagined being here with him under that soft quilt, but he had no way of knowing that.

She folded up her sweater, wondering if she would ever be able to look the man in the eye again.

"It's a long story. Your sons offered to teach me how to ride horses."

"Trevor and Colter."

She finally gathered the courage to lift her gaze to his. "Do you have any other sons?"

"No. Two are enough, thanks. Why would Trevor and Colter offer to teach you how to ride horses?"

She suddenly didn't know how to answer that. He couldn't know the boys wanted to surprise him with a special song for Christmas, that they were bartering services. Telling him about it would completely ruin the surprise, and she wasn't about to do that to the boys, especially after they were trying so hard to uphold their side of the bargain.

"I guess they felt sorry for me when I told them I couldn't ride. I may have let slip at some point that I'm a little...nervous around horses and I would like to get over it."

He raised an eyebrow. "Let me get this straight. You're nervous around horses, but somehow you thought two seven-year-old boys could help you get over your fear?"

Okay, it sounded ridiculous when he said it like that. What had seemed like a good idea at the time now seemed nothing short of foolish.

"Why not? They're excellent riders and their enthusiasm is...contagious."

"Like chicken pox."

"Something like that." She forced a smile. "They aren't afraid to tell everyone what good riders they are. I figured it couldn't hurt to see if some of that enthusiasm might rub off on me."

It sounded silly in retrospect, but there was nothing she could do about that at this point. The deal had been struck and she didn't want to hurt the boys by pulling out of the arrangement now, when they were so excited to teach her.

Beck continued to watch her with a baffled look on

his features. What was he even doing there? She thought he was supposed to be out of town this weekend.

"If you would rather I didn't go riding with them, I understand. I should have asked you first. The boys and I talked about it yesterday after practice. They told me you wouldn't be here but that Dan said it was okay. I guess I assumed perhaps he would talk to you. I don't want to cause trouble, though. If you don't want me here, I can grab my Christmas sweater and go home."

She wouldn't blame the man if he threw her off his ranch. Without telling him about the deal she and the boys struck, she sounded completely irrational.

"No. It's fine. We have a couple of really gentle horses that are good for beginners."

She released the breath she hadn't realized she'd been holding. He didn't *sound* like he thought she was crazy.

"The boys promised me a horse named Creampuff. I like the sound of that name, if she lives up to it."

"That's just the horse I would have suggested. She's about as mellow as it gets."

"Sounds perfect. Thank you."

He tilted his head and studied her. "You can ride our sweet Creampuff on one condition."

"What's that?" she asked, suddenly wary at the look in his eyes.

"You let *me*, not the twins, give you riding lessons."

She instantly remembered standing close to him and the shivery little ache that had spread through her. The more time she spent with Beckett McKinley, the more chance she had of making a complete idiot of herself over him.

"That's completely not necessary," she said quickly. "I'm sure the boys and I will be fine."

"First lesson of horses, you can't be sure of anything. Even the most gentle horse can sometimes be unpredictable. I would hate for something to happen to you." He cleared his throat. "Just like I would hate for something to happen to *anyone* on my ranch, riding one of my horses."

Naturally, he wasn't worrying about her in particular. She told herself that little ache under her breastbone was a hunger pang, nothing more. It certainly wouldn't have been disappointment.

What exactly would riding lessons from Beckett McKinley entail? Did she want to find out?

"The boys were looking forward to teaching me." She tried one last time.

"They can still take the lead and give you some pointers. It will be a good experience for them, actually. I'm sure you've found that teachers often learn more than their students about a subject matter. It's good for them to think about the fundamentals of something that by now seems instinctive to them."

She would have to agree. Teaching someone else how to play a particular instrument always reminded her of the basics.

"They can take the lead but I would feel better if I could be there to keep an eye on things, just in case."

She told herself she didn't want his eyes—or anything else—on her. But what choice did she have? It was his ranch, his sons, his horses.

"I thought you were supposed to be out of town, buying horses."

She didn't want to tell him that she would never have agreed to come here for these lessons if she thought she would run into him. If she had known he would end up finding her half-dressed in his bedroom with a sweater tangled in her hair, she would have locked herself in her own bedroom at the Baker's Dozen.

"Plans changed. We found the horses we needed early on and agreed to a fair price with the owner, so we didn't need to stay for the entire sale. We came back last night."

No doubt that defined most of Beck's life. He made a decision early and then went for it. That was probably fine when it came to horses, but not so good when he made a snap decision about her and couldn't seem to see beyond it.

"You thought I was gone."

"The boys said something about it. I would never have come to your bedroom to change my clothes if I thought there was any chance you could be here to run into me."

"Were you hoping to avoid me?"

"Don't be silly," she snapped. "Why would I need to avoid you?"

He didn't answer, only raised an eyebrow.

Before she could think of a way to answer, she heard one of the twins from outside. It sounded like Trevor, but their voices were so similar, it was tough to tell them apart when she couldn't see them.

"Miss Ella? Is everything okay? Our sandwiches are all done but Uncle Dan says we have to wait for you so we can eat. He said that's the polite thing to do when you have guests."

He sounded so disgusted, she had to smile. "It is customary, yes."

"How much longer is it gonna take you to get dressed?"

He didn't say it outright, but the implication was clear. *What the Sam Hill is taking you so blasted long?*

"I'm ready now. I'm coming," she called, before turning back to Beck. "I'm sorry you were dragged into this when you probably had other things to do this afternoon. I'll make some excuse to the boys, tell them I changed my mind or something."

"Why would you go and do that, especially after we went to all the trouble to get you extricated from your Christmas sweater?"

The man had a point. Something told her she wouldn't be able to wriggle out of these lessons like she had eventually done with her sweater. She was stuck, so she might as well make the best of it.

Chapter Six

After she left, Beck released his breath, then inhaled deeply. The scent of her still filled his bedroom—peaches and cinnamon, a combination that made his mouth water.

How did Ella Baker manage to twist him into a dozen crazy knots every time he was with her? He felt as trussed up as a calf at a roping competition.

He closed his eyes, reliving how stunned he had been to walk into his own bedroom and discover her standing there, half-dressed, like all his illicit fantasies come true.

Okay, she hadn't really been half-dressed. She had been wearing a plain T-shirt, but he wasn't sure if she was aware it had ridden up with the sweater, revealing about three inches of bare, creamy abdomen.

At the sight of that little strip of skin, his stupid brain had taken him in all sorts of unruly directions. He had wanted to kiss that patch of skin, to slide off the rest of her clothes, to toss her down on his bed and spend the rest of the day tangled under the quilt with her.

Man, he had it bad.

He opened his eyes as the magnitude of what he had consented to do loomed suddenly as large as the Tetons outside his windows.

Riding lessons. How in the world was he supposed to give the woman riding lessons, when he couldn't stop thinking about all the inappropriate things he would much rather teach her instead?

And what on earth were his boys thinking, to invite her here without talking to him first? He sighed. Those two rascals had the funniest, most convoluted thought processes, especially when they had their minds set on a project. He supposed he should be happy they liked their music teacher enough to want to help her.

Wasn't that what the holidays were all about? Helping others? He didn't see how he could object, really.

She *did* have a phobia about horses. A fairly serious one. He had seen it for himself one day over the summer, when he had been repairing a fence line between the two ranches. Because it had been a lovely July morning, he'd chosen to ride Ace on a trail that connected the two ranches, to the spot that needed repair. He had been minding his own business, enjoying the splendor of the day, when Ella had suddenly jogged into sight on the trail ahead of him, listening to music through earbuds and wearing shorts that showed off her tanned legs.

She hadn't noticed him at first, probably because of the music. When she spotted him and Ace, she had jumped a mile and had scrambled onto a rock beside the trail to let him pass. He had stopped to greet her—the polite thing to do between neighbors—but she hadn't seemed at all in the mood to chat.

He thought it was because she didn't like him. Now he wondered if it had more to do with her aversion to horses.

He wasn't sure if he and the boys could do anything to help that kind of phobia, but he suddenly wanted to try. He would like to be able to give her this. It was a small thing, only a few hours out of his life, but if he could help her get over her fear of horses, he might feel a little less guilty about taking up Curt on his offer to buy the Baker's Dozen.

It only took a few moments for him to realize the task of helping Ella conquer her fear of horses might be slightly harder than he suspected.

"Nothing to be afraid of." He kept his voice calm, slow, just as he would do to a spooked mare. "Creampuff is as easy and gentle as her name. She's not going to hurt you, I promise. It's not in her nature."

"I'm not afraid," she said, which was an outright lie. Her body betrayed her. She trembled, muscles poised as if she was ready to bolt.

"Sure. I believe you," he said, his voice soothing.

Her nervousness temporarily lifted long enough for her to glare at him. "You don't have to patronize me," she said stiffly. "It must be obvious I'm terrified. I don't want to be, but I am."

"You don't have to be afraid, Miss Ella," Colter told her with an earnest look. "Creampuff is so lazy, she only moves every other Sunday. That's what Dad says, anyway."

"Good thing today is Saturday, then," she said, with a slight smile.

"Exactly," Trevor said. "Why don't you start by making friends with her? Dad keeps crab apples in the barn for her, since that's her favorite treat."

That was a good idea to break the ice between her and the horse, one he should have thought of himself. His boys were smart little caballeros.

"Colt, why don't you grab a couple? You remember how to open the box?"

"Yep." Colter headed over to the metal box containing the treat. "We had to put a latch on it after Creampuff here learned how to lift the lid and help herself."

"Did she?" Ella's voice was faint, as if coming from the other side of the barn.

"She would eat those until she's sick, unless we put a few obstacles in her way," Beck answered, still in that calming voice. "Here you are. Give her this, nice and slow."

He handed her a crab apple. "Put it on your palm, not your fingers." He probably shouldn't tell her that if she wasn't careful, Creampuff might munch on her fingers by mistake.

"There. She likes you," he said when the horse lipped the apple from her palm. He also didn't mention that Creampuff would take a crab apple from just about anybody or anything. She had no scruples when it came to her treats.

"How about another?" he asked. Without waiting for an answer, he handed her a second crab apple. She put it on her palm herself and actually smiled a little this time when Creampuff snatched it away before she could even thrust her hand out all the way.

"Now pet her," Trevor suggested. "She likes it when you scratch along her neck. Yep, like that."

"You must think I'm the world's biggest scaredy-cat."

His boys didn't say anything. Though no one could ever call them well-mannered, precisely, sometimes they could be surprisingly polite. This was one of those times. They looked at each other but chose to remain silent rather than agree with her.

"I don't think you're a scaredy-cat," Beck said quietly. "I think something terrible must have happened to you on a horse."

She sent him a swift look, and he could see the truth of his words reflected in the haunted shadows in her gaze. "How did you know? Did my father tell you?"

It didn't exactly take a crack detective to figure it out. She wasn't just nervous, she was petrified.

This hadn't been a good idea. He didn't like seeing her so upset.

"You don't have to do this, you know. There's no law that says you have to ride horses around here."

She was silent, petting the horse. He was happy to see her hands weren't trembling quite as much as they had earlier.

"You might not find it in any Pine Gulch city code," she said after a moment, "but it's one of those unwritten societal laws, understood by everyone who lives here. You have to know your way around horses if you want to truly fit in around here."

He opened his mouth to argue with her, then closed it again. There might be a kernel of truth to what she said, at least in some circles. He had a feeling Curt Baker saw things that way. He was an old-school rancher, through and through. Funny that Curt himself didn't ride, either. Beck had to wonder if that had something to do with whatever had happened to Ella.

"I've always figured most rules were made just so folks could figure out a creative way to break them. Really, Ella. Don't torture yourself. It's not worth it"

She gazed at him, eyes wide as if she didn't expect understanding from him. Her surprise made him squirm. What? He could be as sensitive as the next guy.

She looked at him, then at Creampuff. As he watched, determination flooded those blue eyes.

"I want to do this. I can't let my fear of something that happened when I was eight years old control the rest of my life," she said. "I've given it too much power already."

Eight years old. He tried to picture her, pigtailed and cute and blonde, with that little hint of freckles. What had frightened her so badly?

Whatever it was, he respected the hell out of her for her courage in confronting it.

"Okay, then." His voice came out more gruffly than usual. "Now that you've made friends with Creampuff here, I guess it's time to climb on. When you're ready, I'll give you a hand."

Her hands clenched into fists at her side then unclenched and she nodded. "I'm ready."

Filled with admiration—not to mention this blasted attraction he didn't want—he helped her hold on to the saddle horn and put her boot in the stirrup, then gave her a lift into the saddle.

She held tight to the horn. "I forgot how far off the ground I can feel on the back of a horse."

The twins had mounted by themselves and rode their horses closer to her. "It's great, isn't it?" Trevor said with a grin. "I feel about eight feet tall when I'm on Oreo."

She seemed to be close to hyperventilating. They

couldn't have that. He stepped closer and kept his voice low and calming.

"Just hold on to the reins. I've hooked a lead line here and I'm just going to walk you around the training arena a bit, until you feel more comfortable."

"You won't let go?" Her panic was palpable.

He gave her a reassuring smile. "I promise. You got this."

As he led her around the small arena where they held horse auctions and worked to train horses in bad weather, he kept talking in that slow voice about nothing, really. The year he constructed this building, the other barn that was built by his great-grandfather, the house his grandfather had added.

The boys could never have handled this level of fear. He was deeply grateful that his schedule had worked out so he could be here to help her through this.

"You're doing great," he said after about fifteen minutes, when she seemed to have relaxed a little and her features no longer looked so pinched and pale. "You ready to take the reins on your own now?"

"Do I have to?" she asked ruefully. "I was just beginning to breathe again."

He tried to hide his smile. She had grit. He'd give her that. "You don't have to, but you'll never really get a feel for riding a horse until you're the one in command."

She released a heavy sigh. "I suppose you're right. Okay. You can let go."

He twisted the lead line onto the saddle horn and stood by her thigh. "Here are a few basics. Sit up tall, creating a nice, straight line from shoulders to hips. Don't hold the reins taut, just relax them in your hands, and use the least amount of pressure you can to get the horse to do what you want. It's all about pressure and release. The moment she starts doing what you want, going where you want, you let off the pressure."

He went over a few other basic commands but he could see Ella was starting to glaze over.

For all her complacency, Creampuff was a very well-trained horse. She tended to know what her rider wanted before the rider did.

"You got this," he repeated, then stood back to watch.

Ella sat atop the motionless horse for a long moment, then—just as he was about to step in and give Creampuff a verbal command—Ella gave the perfect amount of pressure with her knees into her sides to get her moving.

Though her movements were awkward and stiff, she had obviously been on a horse before. He was a fairly decent teacher but not *that* good that she could instantly pick it up. No, he had a feeling it was more a case of muscle memory. Ella held the reins in the best position and didn't yank them, but instead used slow, steady movements.

She had done this before. Even if it was a long time ago, something inside her remembered.

Colter and Trevor watched from the back of their horses. "You're doing great," Trevor called.

"Keep it up," his brother said. "Way to go, Miss Ella. You'll be riding the rodeo before you know it."

Ella's visible shudder at the suggestion might have made him smile under other circumstances, if he wasn't so worried about her.

"You *are* doing great," he called. "Now see if you can get her to go a little faster."

"Why on earth would I do that? I don't *want* her to go faster."

He tipped his hat back. "Okay. Take it slow and steady. Nothing wrong with that."

She kept going another twenty minutes, taking the horse around the arena several times, then practicing bringing her a stop again before urging her forward once more. By the time they were done and she rode to a stop in front of him, she looked exhausted but beautifully triumphant.

"You ready to call it a day?"

"Yes. I think so."

He reached up a hand to help her and as she slid off the horse and to the ground, he tried not to notice how wonderful her soft curves felt against him. He was quick to let go when her boots hit the dirt floor.

"How was it?" he asked.

"Not as difficult as I expected, actually." She looked surprised and rather pleased at that discovery. "You were right. Creampuff really is a sweetheart."

"She does live up to her name, doesn't she?" He gave the old horse an appreciative pat as the twins rode up and dismounted.

"You did super good," Colter said.

"Yeah," his brother agreed. "You hardly even bounced around in the saddle."

"I hate to admit it, but there is a certain part of me that would disagree with you right now," Ella said, rubbing the back pocket of her jeans.

The boys giggled while Beck did his best not to shift his gaze to that particular portion of her anatomy.

"Boys, can you take care of the horses? Miss Baker's, too."

The twins had been brushing down their horses since they were old enough to ride. They led the horses away and he turned to Ella, though he kept one eye on the boys, across the arena, as they scrambled to take off saddles and hackamores. They didn't need direct supervision but he still liked to monitor things in case they had trouble.

"That was some good, hard work. A lesson like that deserves a beer. Or at least a soda."

"I wouldn't mind some water," she said.

"I don't doubt it. Overcoming your fear is thirsty business."

In the harsh lights of the indoor arena, her color rose and she looked down.

"Hey. I meant that with upmost respect," he assured her. He led the way into the corner that functioned as the office out here. He reached into the fridge and pulled out a water bottle for her, a beer for him.

"You really did work hard. I could tell it wasn't easy for you."

She sighed and took a healthy swallow from the bottle. A few little droplets clung to her lips from the bottle's mouth and he had to fight the urge to press his own lips there.

"It's so stupid," she said, frustration simmering in her voice. "I don't know why I can't get past it."

"Want to tell me about it?"

She looked at the horses, then back at him with a helpless sort of look. "Not really. But I suppose you have the right to know, especially after all your help this afternoon."

"I don't know about that. But I'd like to hear, if you want to tell me."

She took another swallow and he had the feeling she was biding time as much as slaking her thirst. "You know I didn't grow up on the Baker's Dozen."

Considering he had lived next to Curt his whole life and only saw Ella a few memorable times over the years, until she moved back to Pine Gulch, he was aware of that fact. "I did. I gather your parents were divorced."

"Yes. Eventually. They were separated on and off through most of my early childhood. They would try to make it work for a month or two, usually for my sake, then things would go south and my mom would pack us up and move back to Boston."

"That must have been tough."

"Yes. I adored my father and I always loved coming out to the ranch, even when it was just for a short visit. My favorite times were the summers, when I could be here for weeks at a time. Back in Boston, I dreamed about horses all the time. In the pictures I've seen of my bedroom, there are dozens of pictures on the wall of horses I had either drawn myself or cut out of old ranch magazines I took back with me. I loved to ride. At least that's what they tell me."

That struck him as an odd way to phrase things, but she continued before he could ask what she meant.

"I was three the first time my dad put me on a horse. I don't have a memory of it. Or anything else before I was eight years old."

That seemed awfully late for a first memory.

"Eight? Why eight?"

She looked down at her water bottle with a faraway expression. When she looked back up at him, her expression was bleak.

"That's the year I died."

Chapter Seven

Died? What the hell was that supposed to mean? Shock tangled his tongue, but even if it hadn't, he would have had no idea how to respond.

"I know. That sounds ridiculous and melodramatic," she said, her expression rueful. "But it's the truth. I was dead for about five minutes before they could get my heart started again."

She spoke in a matter-of-fact way, but her hands trembled again, as they had when she first faced the horse arena.

"You were eight? What happened?"

She watched the boys as they competently brushed down the horses. "My mom and I were both here that summer. It was the last time my parents tried to reconcile, I guess, though they didn't tell me that was why we had come back to the ranch. They had been separated on and off most of my life, but neither of them could ever bring themselves to file for divorce. I don't know why but they couldn't seem to take that final step."

"Were you happy about it? About your parents trying to reconcile?"

"I wish I could tell you. Apparently I wanted nothing more than to live here permanently. According to my mom, all I talked about whenever we were in Boston was living here in Pine Gulch and having my own horse and riding whenever I wanted. I think she resented how much I loved the ranch, if you want the truth. She never did."

Yet one more thing he had in common with Curt Baker. The man had never come right out and said it, but Beck had guessed as much.

What was wrong with these Pine Gulch men who insisted on marrying completely inappropriate women who couldn't wait to leave?

"We had only been back about three weeks when I took out a new horse," Ella went on. "I was with my dad and we were just riding above the ranch, nothing too strenuous, but apparently a snake slithered across the trail and spooked the horse and I fell—not just off the horse but about twenty feet down a rocky slope. I ended up with multiple injuries."

His blood ran cold as he pictured it. "You stopped breathing, you said?"

"Yes. My father was right there and he managed to do CPR to eventually restart my heart. I was airlifted to the hospital in Idaho Falls, and then to the regional children's hospital in Salt Lake City."

"How long were you there?"

"Two months. Seven surgeries. I was in a medically induced coma for weeks while the swelling from the brain injury went down. When I came out of it, there was obvious damage. I didn't remember anything. Not just the accident, but everything that happened before. Total blank slate. I had to relearn how to walk, talk, use a fork. Everything. I still have no memory of what happened the first eight years of my life, only from pictures and what my parents have told me."

He shook his head, trying to imagine how tough that must have been, to lose eight years of her life. He glanced at the boys, who were just finishing up with Creampuff. She was only a little older than they were and had to relearn everything.

No wonder she had been terrified of horses! He wasn't sure he ever would have had the guts to get back on.

"I just have one question."

"What's that?"

His jaw clenched. "Why in *blazes* did you get back on a horse today, after everything you've been through? I would think any sane woman would try to stay as far away as possible from something that's caused so much suffering."

She looked pensive, her fingers curled around the water bottle. "Today wasn't about the horses, Beck. It was about me." She paused. "I keep thinking that if I learn how to ride again, I'll find some piece of me I lost when I was eight."

He couldn't believe Curt had never told him about Ella's accident. Maybe that explained why the man didn't have any horses on the Baker's Dozen. He knew some ranchers thought they were too much trouble and not worth the effort, preferring ATVs and utility vehicles to a good cattle horse. He had always assumed Curt was one of them.

"I guess your parents didn't get back together."

She gave a short laugh. "You could say that. My mother would have been happy if I never came back to Pine Gulch. She blamed my father, said Curt deliberately put me on a horse that wasn't appropriate for an eight-year-old girl with limited experience who wasn't the expert rider she thought she was. She filed for divorce while I was still in the hospital."

How had that impacted Ella? Did she blame herself for her parents' divorce? Did she wonder if they would have been able to finally piece things together, if not for her fall?

He couldn't help seeing her with new compassion and found himself impressed all over again at the courage it must have taken her today to climb up on Creampuff.

"For the first few years after the divorce, she made my dad fly out to Boston for visits, which he hated. They were awkward, tense episodes that weren't comfortable for either of us. When I got older, after the dust from their custody battle settled, I insisted on coming out as often as I could. My dad refused to let me get on a horse. To reduce temptation, he sold them all, even though it was something he always loved. That was a tough pill for me to swallow, but Curt said my mom wouldn't let me come back to the ranch if she found out I had gone riding again. He wasn't wrong, actually."

He couldn't imagine that kind of animosity. Beck's own parents had been happily married until his father's untimely death, even with his mom's rheumatoid arthritis, which limited what she could do around the ranch. His dad had been a loving caretaker as far back as Beck could remember, one of the things he respected most about him.

After his father died, Beck's mother had moved to

Florida to be closer to her sister. She was doing well there, though he missed her. She and the boys talked via Skype every Sunday evening.

"I can't believe I didn't know this about you," he finally said.

She made a wry face. "It's not like I go around introducing myself to people by telling them that I spent several weeks in a medically induced coma after falling off a horse."

"But my family lived next door to yours. I should have known. I would have been, what, eleven or twelve? That's old enough to be aware of what's going on in my own community."

On the other hand, Curt Baker had always been a little removed from the greater Pine Gulch society. Beck's parents may well have known and may have mentioned it to him, but since he didn't know Ella personally back then and she was several years younger—and a girl, to boot— he wasn't sure it would have had much impact on him.

"It doesn't matter," she said. "It was a long time ago. Almost twenty years. The doctors all said it was a miracle that I made it through without much lasting damage."

"Nothing?"

"My leg aches in bad weather and I still limp a bit when I'm tired. To be totally honest, I do have the occasional memory lapse. I call it a glitch. Every once in a while, I forget a word that's pretty basic."

"Everybody does that."

"That's what I tell myself. I'm lucky. It could have been much worse."

"It doesn't sound like nothing. It sounds like you've been through hell. Nobody would blame you for never getting on a horse again, Ella. Like I said, it's really not necessary out here. There are plenty of people in Pine Gulch who've never been on a horse yet somehow still manage to live good, productive lives."

She was quiet, her features pensive. "I hate being afraid," she finally said. "Especially of something I once loved."

He had to respect that. "I'm not sure you can force yourself to the other side of a perfectly justifiable fear, simply through willpower."

"Maybe not completely," she acknowledged. "I'm okay with that. Still, I'd like to see if I can regain a little of that passion I once had."

He wanted that for her, too. In that moment, Beck resolved to do whatever he could to help her. "In that case, you'd better come back tomorrow for a second lesson. One hour in a horse arena on the back of a narcoleptic nag like Creampuff isn't enough to inspire passion in anyone."

"I don't know about that. I enjoyed myself far more than I expected."

"Come back tomorrow. Let's see if you can enjoy it even more."

"I could do that." She considered. "It would actually be good timing. Some friends are taking my father to a cowboy poetry event in Idaho Falls and they're supposed to be gone most of the day."

"You're a grown woman, Ella. He can't stop you from riding now, even if he wanted to."

"I know. I usually make him a nice dinner on Sunday afternoons after church. Since he'll be gone, I won't have to do that—or explain why I'm leaving or where I'm going."

"Great. You can just come straight here after church,

then. You might as well stay for dinner. We'll probably grill steaks. It's just as easy to toss another one on the coals."

He wasn't sure why he extended the invitation. By her expression, it was clear she was as shocked as he was by it.

"I... Thank you. That would be nice. I'll bring a salad and rolls and some kind of dessert."

"You don't have to do that, but I'm sure the boys would enjoy it."

His side dishes usually consisted of baked potatoes or instant rice.

"Enjoy what?" Trevor asked. They had apparently finished with the horses, who were all fed and watered and turned out to pasture.

"Miss Baker is going to come for another riding lesson tomorrow. I invited her to have dinner with us, too."

"Yay!" Trevor exclaimed.

Colter, he noticed with sudden trepidation, was giving the two of them a speculative look that left Beck more than a little uncomfortable.

What was going through the kid's mind? Beck wasn't sure he wanted to know—any more than he wanted to examine his own thoughts, at least about Ella Baker.

She wasn't sure she should be doing this.

Even as she loaded food into her SUV in preparation for driving back to the Broken Arrow, Ella was filled with misgivings.

She still had no idea what had prompted Beck to issue this unexpected invitation to dinner and a second riding lesson. Maybe pity. He *had* invited her right after she spilled her entire pathetic story to the man, after all.

More puzzling than his invitation had been how quickly she accepted it, without really thinking things through.

She should have refused. As much as she might have wanted another lesson, another chance to recapture the joy she had once known while riding, she was beginning to think it might not be a good idea to spend more time with Beckett and his boys.

The lesson the day before had eroded her defenses, left her far too open and vulnerable to him. She rarely talked about her accident, even with close friends. It was a part of her, yes, but something that happened so long ago, it hardly seemed relevant to the woman she had become—except as it pertained to her lingering fear of horses.

Why had she confided in Beckett McKinley, of all people?

He had been so patient with her during the lesson and, dare she say, even kind. It was a side of him she wasn't used to seeing. She could admit, she found it wildly appealing.

She wished she could have been able to tell what had been running through his mind when she told him what had happened so long ago. No such luck. The man was still a mystery to her. Every time she thought she had him figured out, he did something to toss all her preconceptions out the window.

This invitation for dinner, for instance. It would have been kind enough to simply invite her over for the lesson. Why add dinner into the mix?

Maybe he just felt sorry for her. The poor, pathetic girl who had nearly died not far from here.

She sighed and climbed into the SUV. She didn't like that idea. But what else could it be?

Though she was tempted to call off the whole thing, she made herself drive through the lightly falling snow to the nearby ranch.

The snowflakes looked lovely as they twirled out of the sky against the pine trees that bordered the road. The perfect holiday scene—except this was her second winter in southern Idaho and she knew the winters here could be anything but idyllic.

Oh, she hoped the weather cooperated for the Christmas program the following week. The children had already worked so hard to learn the songs and would be putting in a full week of intense rehearsals. She hated to think of all their effort being wasted because bad weather kept people away.

That was a hazard of living here, she supposed. You just had to keep your fingers crossed and learn how to take what comes.

Her stomach knotted with nerves as she drove under the Broken Arrow arch, which also had their brand burned into it. She had seen the McKinley men only hours ago at church. Beck had looked big and tough and handsome in his bolo tie and western-cut suit and the boys had looked just as handsome in clean white shirts and similar bolo ties.

They had come in late, hair still wet and Trevor's shirt buttoned wrong, and had waved so enthusiastically at her as they took their seats that Celeste Delaney beside her had whispered a teasing comment about the McKinley twin terrors having a crush on her.

She hadn't responded, even though she wanted to tell Celeste they weren't terrors. They were sweet, good-hearted boys who happened to have a little more energy than most.

She wasn't sure how her feelings for the boys had shifted so abruptly after only a few encounters. A week ago, she would have been one of those rolling her eyes at their antics. Now she saw them through a new filter of affection and even tenderness.

Mostly, they needed a little more direction and restraint in their lives.

She pulled up to the ranch house, her pulse abnormally loud in her ears, aware it wasn't the horse riding that made her nervous this time, but the idea of spending an afternoon with Beck and his adorable sons.

It was too late to back out now, she told herself, as she headed up the porch steps and rang the doorbell. They were planning on her.

Colter answered before the doorbell even stopped echoing through the house.

"Hey, Miss Ella!" he exclaimed, giving her that irresistible gap-toothed grin. "Guess what? Our dog is having puppies, *right now.*"

"Is that right?"

"Yeah. She's down in the barn. Dad says we can go down to see her again after you get here."

Beck walked into the foyer in time to hear his son's announcement. He looked gorgeous and relaxed in jeans and a casual collared navy shirt that made his eyes gleam an even deeper blue.

"More excitement than you were probably expecting on a quiet Sunday afternoon."

As if she needed more excitement than the anticipation bubbling through her all morning at the idea of spending the afternoon with him and his boys.

"I would love to see the puppies, if you don't think the mother would mind."

"This is her fifth litter. At this point, I don't think she would care if the high school marching band came through during labor."

She couldn't hide her smile at that image. For a moment, something hot and glittery flashed in Beck's expression as he gazed down at her. Her resident butterfly friends danced harder in her stomach.

He seemed to have lost his cool politeness toward her and she didn't know whether to be relieved or terrified.

She was already ridiculously attracted to him, on a purely physical level. She would be in serious trouble if she actually *liked* him, too.

Something told her it was a little too late for caution now.

After a moment, he cleared his throat. "We can take a look on our way down to the horse barn."

"Sounds good. I have a salad that needs to go in the refrigerator and rolls that will need to continue rising. Mind if I put them in your kitchen first?"

"If it means fresh rolls, you can do anything you want."

Ella was quite certain he didn't mean the words in any suggestible way. That didn't stop her imagination from going a little wild for just a moment, until she reined it back with much more pressure than she would ever have used on Creampuff.

"This way," he said.

She followed him into his updated kitchen, with its stainless appliances and granite countertops.

The day before, when she'd eaten lunch here, she had observed that this was obviously a household of men. The kitchen wasn't messy, exactly, but it was more cluttered than she personally would have found comfortable. The sink had dishes left over from breakfast, and some kind of dried substance, likely from an overflowing pasta pot, covered one of the burners.

Just like the day before, she had a strong impulse to dig in and go to work cleaning things up, but she had to remind herself that wasn't her bailiwick. She was only there for dinner and another riding lesson.

"Sorry about the mess in here." Beck looked a little uncomfortable. "Until a few months ago, we had a nanny-slash-housekeeper, but she was having some health problems so had to take a break. My brother and uncle and I have been trading off household responsibilities until I can find someone new and I'm afraid none of us is very good at it."

The picture touched her, three men working together to take care of these twin boys. She remembered Faith telling her Beck had refused to give his in-laws custody, though the boys had only been toddlers.

Ella was aware of a small, soft warmth fluttering to life in her chest.

"It's a lovely home," she murmured. "I can tell the boys are very happy here."

He offered that rare smile again and for a moment, she felt as if that warmth was swirling between the two of them, urging them inexorably closer.

"I should put this in the refrigerator," she said quickly, holding out the bowl containing the green salad she had made.

"Let me make a little room." He moved a few things around, leaving her a space amongst a few leftover containers and a half-empty case of beer.

"Now I only need a warm spot for the rolls to rise. Any suggestions?"

"Judy, our old housekeeper, always used the laundry room."

"That works."

He led the way to a large combined mudroom and laundry room. There were two washers and dryers in the space and both were going, sending out humid heat that would be perfect for her wrap-covered rolls.

"Judy always used that shelf up there. It's a little high for you to reach, I can put them up there for you."

"Looks like a perfect spot. Thanks." She handed him the jelly-roll pan of dough balls. Their fingers touched as he took it from her and a shiver rippled over her.

She thought his gaze sharpened but she couldn't be sure. Oh, she hoped he didn't notice her unwilling reaction.

He took the pan but simply held it for a long moment as the tension seemed to thicken between them. He looked as if he had something he wanted to say and even opened his mouth, but the boys burst into the laundry room before he could.

Ella told herself she was relieved.

"Let's go! We want to see the puppies!" Colter said, voice brimming with excitement.

Beck finally looked away to focus on his sons. "We're coming. Grab your coats while you're in here."

The boys complied and Beck finally slid the pan of rolls onto the high shelf, where the warmth would help them rise more quickly.

"How long until they're ready to bake?"

"I pulled the dough out of the freezer, so it will need to thaw as well as rise. Probably about ninety minutes."

Her dad loved homemade rolls, but it was too much trouble to do very often for only the two of them, so she had started making a big batch every month and freezing the dough.

"That should be about perfect to give us time to see the puppies and ride for a while, if you're still up for it."

"I'm here, aren't I?" she said wryly. "I'm ready."

"Excellent. Let's go."

The twins led the way outside, chattering to each other about Christmas vacation and a school field trip during the upcoming week to The Christmas Ranch, where they both planned to visit Sparkle, the famous reindeer immortalized in books as well as onscreen in an animated movie.

She would have thought their daily rehearsals at the ranch were sufficient holiday cheer, but apparently not.

By default, she and Beckett fell behind the boys a little.

"How's your dad?" Beck said. "I haven't seen him for a few days."

She sighed with remembered frustration. Curt was having a hard time accepting his limitations. That morning, before he left for the cowboy poetry event, she had caught him trying to put up a stepladder to fix a lightbulb that had gone out in their great room. The man had poor balance on solid ground, forget about eight feet up in the air on a wobbly ladder.

"Stubborn as ever," she answered. "I'm beginning to think it must be something in the water up here."

He laughed, the sound rich and deep in the cold December air. "You might be right about that. I've got two boys drinking that same water and they could write the book on stubborn."

He definitely had his hands full with those twins. She

had a feeling things weren't going to get easier as they hit their preteen and teenage years.

"Anyway, your dad might be stubborn but he's a good man. After my dad died when I was still too young to know what the hell I was doing here on the ranch, Curt took me under his wing. I learned more from him those first few months than my whole twenty-three years before that."

She hadn't realized his father died when Beck was so young. Sympathy for him helped mute the sting of hearing her father had been willing to help a neighbor learn the ropes of ranching. Too bad he wouldn't do the same thing for his own daughter.

"What happened to your father?"

"One of those freak things. Doctors figured it was a brain aneurysm. He was out on a tractor, perfectly fine one minute, the next he was gone. I'd always planned to take over the Broken Arrow from him, since neither of my brothers was much interested in running the place."

"Jax works here, doesn't he?"

"Yeah, but it took him a while to figure out what he wanted to do. I'm still not convinced his heart's in it, but it's tough to tell with Jax. I always knew I wanted to run the ranch, I just didn't expect to do it so early."

"I'm sorry. That must have been tough on you."

"At first, but good neighbors like Curt stepped in to help me figure things out."

"I'm glad my dad was here for you," she said softly. "And now you're helping him in return."

Beck shrugged, looking embarrassed. "I'm not doing much. I'm glad I can help."

He stopped in front of a different barn than the larger, more modern facility where they had ridden the day before. "Here we are. Guys, remember what I told you. We can watch, if we do it quietly so we don't distract Sal while she's taking care of her puppies."

"We remember," Trevor said solemnly. The boys tiptoed into the barn—which wasn't particularly effective, since they were both wearing cowboy boots.

She followed, not sure what to expect. The barn was warmer than she might have thought, and smelled of straw and old wood and the earthy smells she associated with a ranch.

Beck led the way to a wooden stall about halfway back. She peered over the railing to where a mostly black border collie lay on her side on a blanket that had been spread over the straw.

She looked exhausted, poor thing, as her litter suckled for nourishment.

"They look like little rats," Trevor whispered.

"Beautiful little rats," his brother said loyally, which made Ella smile.

The puppies were small, eyes still closed. They made little whiny noises as they ate.

"Is that all of them, girl?" Beck asked in a low voice. "Looks like she might be done. How many do you count?"

"Seven," Colter said, moving his finger in the air to mark each one. "No, eight."

"Good job, Sal," Beck said softly. The tired mother gave a half-hearted tail wag before returning to care for her litter.

They all watched the little creatures with fascination for a few more moments. It was an unexpectedly intimate moment, standing there by the wooden stall beside Beck and his boys, almost like they were a family unit.

They most definitely weren't, she reminded herself. That sort of thinking could get her into all kinds of trouble.

"We should probably let her rest now," Beck said eventually.

"Will they all be okay out here?" Trevor asked. "It's cold outside."

"But warm in here. Sal and the puppies have everything they need here—warm, soft blankets, with plenty for Sal to eat and drink. My guess is, she'll probably want to sleep for a week after having eight puppies."

"What will you do with them all?" Ella asked.

"I'll probably keep a couple to train, then sell the others. Sal has champion bloodlines and the sire does, too. Those are going to be some excellent cow dogs."

He glanced down at her. "You ready to ride again?"

"I am," she admitted. "Believe it or not, I'm actually looking forward to it."

He gave her a full-on, high-octane smile that turned her insides to rich, gooey honey.

"That is an excellent sign, Miss Baker. Watch and see. We'll make a horsewoman out of you yet."

She didn't share his confidence—but as long as she no longer had panic attacks when she came within a hundred feet of a horse, she would consider these few days to be worth it.

Chapter Eight

An hour later, she managed to pull Creampuff to a stop squarely in front of the spot at the railing where Beck had stood for the last hour, offering advice and encouragement during the lesson.

"Good girl," she said, patting the horse's withers.

"Wait, was that an actual smile?" he teased. "If I didn't know better, I might think you're enjoying yourself."

"You might be right. I think I've almost stopped shaking. That's a good sign, isn't it?"

"An excellent one." He offered an encouraging smile. "On a day when it's not so cold, you should come out to take a trail ride above the house. It's slow going in the snow, but worth it for the views."

A few days earlier, the very idea would have sent her into a panic attack. Her accident had happened in those very foothills and while she didn't remember it, the specter of what had happened there still loomed large in her subconscious.

The fact that she could even consider such an outing was amazing progress. She shifted in the saddle, satisfaction bubbling through her. She had done it, survived another riding lesson, and had actually begun to enjoy the adventure.

Oh, she had missed this. She really did feel as if she was rediscovering a part of herself that had been buried under the rubble of her accident.

Trevor rode up on his big horse, so loose and comfortable that he seemed to be part of the horse. "Is it time for dinner yet? I'm starving."

"Me, too," his brother said, joining the group.

"I guess that's up to our guest," Beck said. "What do you say, Ella? Want to keep riding or would you like to stop for chow?"

"Let's eat, before you guys start chewing the leather reins."

The boys giggled with delight at her lame joke and warmth soaked through her. There was something so *joyful* about being able to make a child laugh. She had never realized that until going to work in music therapy.

"Chew the reins," Trevor said, shaking his head. "That would taste gross!"

"Yeah, steaks would be much better, all the way around," Beck said. "Why don't you boys take care of the horses and put them up while Miss Baker and I start dinner?"

She slid down without assistance. "I would like to help with the horses, actually. If I intend to start riding again, I need to relearn how to care for them."

His eyes warmed with approval. "Good point. It

should only take the four of us a few moments. Boys, let's show Miss Baker how it's done."

Beck couldn't remember the last time he had enjoyed an afternoon so much.

He was growing increasingly intrigued with Ella Baker, forced to completely reevaluate his preconceptions of her as just one more city girl who didn't belong.

She had far more grit than he ever would have believed a few days earlier. Most women who had gone through an ordeal like hers would have stayed as far away as possible from something that represented the trauma they had endured.

Not Ella.

When they had first come into the stables, he had seen how nervous she was. Her small, curvy frame had been trembling slightly as he helped her mount Creampuff, her features pale and set.

It had concerned him a little, especially after she seemed to have enjoyed it the day before. He supposed he should have anticipated her reaction. She had spent many years being afraid of horses, for legitimate reasons. He couldn't expect that to go away overnight, simply because she had an enjoyable experience on an easy mount.

He shouldn't have worried. Within a few moments, she had warmed to it again. After only a few moments, she had visibly relaxed, and by the end of the hour, she had been laughing.

Would she be afraid the next time? For her sake, he hoped she didn't have to fight that battle each time she wanted to ride a horse—though he had to admire the sheer guts she showed by putting herself through it. In his experience, few people demonstrated that kind of raw courage.

He liked her.

Entirely too much.

He frowned at the thought as he hung up the tack on the well-organized pegs. It was hard *not* to like her. She was kind to his sons, she had given up her life back east to come back and care for her father, and she had more courage than most people he'd ever met.

If he wasn't careful, he would do something really stupid, like fall hard for her.

He jerked his mind away from that dangerous possibility. He couldn't. She might be pretty and smart and courageous, but that didn't make her right for him. He would do well to remember she was a city girl. Like her own mother, like Stephanie. Ella was cultured, sophisticated, not the sort of woman who would be comfortable wearing jeans and boots and listening to old Johnny Cash songs.

The thought depressed him more than it should.

They could be friends, though. Nothing wrong with that. A guy couldn't have too many friends, right?

"Everybody ready to go get some food, now that we've all taken care of the horses?" he asked, forcing a note of cheerfulness he didn't feel into his voice.

"Me!" his twins said in unison. Ella smiled and the impact of it was like standing in the middle of a sunbeam.

"We should probably check on the puppies one more time before we head up to the house, if you don't mind," he said.

"Do you seriously think I would mind being able to see those cute puppies again?"

"Good point," he admitted.

The temperature had dropped several degrees by the time they walked outside toward the barn where he had set up Sal for her first few weeks postdelivery. His instincts, honed from years of working the land, warned him they would have snow before morning.

As they trudged through the snow already on the ground from previous storms, he went through his mental weather-preparedness checklist. It wasn't all that lengthy. From his father, he'd learned the important lesson that it was better to ready things well in advance. The Broken Arrow was always set up to deal with bad weather, which made it much easier for this particular ranch owner to sleep at night.

When he wasn't having completely inappropriate dreams about his lovely neighbor, anyway.

In contrast to the gathering storm, the old barn was warm and cozy, a refuge from the Idaho winter.

Sal and her puppies were all sleeping when they peered over the top railing of the stall. Despite Colter's and Trevor's careful effort to tiptoe in on their cowboy boots, Sal must have sensed them. She opened one eye but closed it quickly, busy with the task of keeping eight puppies fed and alive.

Without being asked, Trevor and Colter filled her water and added a bit more food to her bowl. They were such good boys. Yeah, they could be rambunctious at times, but beneath all that energy, they were turning into helpful, compassionate young men.

He couldn't have asked for more.

"She looks exhausted, poor thing," Ella said beside him, her expression soft and sympathetic.

"She's a good mom. She'll be okay after a little rest."

"Until she has eight wriggling puppies climbing all over her."

He grinned. "Shh. Don't say that too loudly or she might decide to hightail it out of here before we get to that point. I don't particularly fancy hand-feeding eight puppies."

"Would she do that?" Ella asked, plainly concerned.

"I'm teasing," he assured her. "Sal knows what to do."

They watched the puppies for a few more moments in silence before he ushered everyone back out into the cold.

"Race you," Trevor said to his brother and the two of them rushed away through the gathering darkness.

"I wish I had even a tiny portion of their energy," Ella said with a sigh.

"Right?"

She shook her head. "How do you keep up with them?"

"Who says I do? There have been more than a few nights when I fall asleep reading to them and only wake up when the book falls to the floor."

She smiled, probably thinking he was kidding. He only wished he were.

"They're good boys. You know that, right?"

He was touched that her thoughts so clearly echoed his own from a few moments earlier. "I do. Once in a while I forget. Like whenever I go to their parent-teacher conferences and hear the litany of classroom complaints. I have to remind myself I wasn't the most patient student, either, yet somehow I still managed to graduate from high school *and* college. My senior year, I was running the ranch, too, and taking night classes."

"It must be challenging on your own."

"Sometimes," he admitted. "There are days I feel like throwing in the parenting towel before we even finish breakfast. It's hard and frustrating and relentless. Each decision I make in the day has to focus on the boys' welfare first. Every other priority is a distant second."

"I can't even imagine." In the fading afternoon light, her features looked soft and so lovely, he had a hard time looking away.

"I'm not really alone, though. Until a few months ago, we had Judy to help us. She did all the heavy lifting when it came to the logistics of caring for the boys when they were smaller."

"You must miss her terribly."

"Definitely. She had been a huge part of our lives since the boys were small. Judy was just about the only mother figure they had. They don't seem to remember their mother much."

"How old were they when she…left?"

He hated thinking about Stephanie and all the mistakes he had made.

"Barely two," he said, his voice pitched low even though the boys had already made it inside.

"She had terrible clinical and postpartum depression as well as anxiety—made harder because, as it turns out, she hated living on a ranch. She missed her family, her friends, the excitement of her life back east."

Their marriage had been an epic mistake from the beginning. He thought they could make a go of things, though now that idea seemed laughable. Still, they had been wildly in love at first. After only a few fiery months, reality had begun to sink in that maybe they couldn't manage to reconcile their differences and then Stephanie found out she was pregnant.

She had cried and cried. He should have clued in to the challenges ahead when he saw her reaction. As for

Beck, he had been scared witless one moment, filled with jubilation the next. He had asked her to marry him and it had taken another three months of discussions—and the revelation through her first ultrasound that her pregnancy would provide a double blessing—before she agreed.

Things only went downhill from there, unfortunately. She had struggled fiercely with postpartum depression and hadn't really bonded with the twins. Even before she left to find help, he and the series of nannies he hired until they found Judy had been the ones getting up at night with them, making sure they were fed, providing the cuddles and the love their mother couldn't.

"That must have been tough," Ella said softly.

For both of them. Stephanie had been a mess emotionally and mentally and he had hated knowing he couldn't fix things for her.

"She stuck it out as long as she could, until both of us realized things weren't getting better. She needed help, more help than she could find here. Her parents are both doctors and had connections back east so they wanted her to get help there. It was always supposed to be temporary but the weeks turned into months and then a year. *Soon*, she kept telling me. Just another month and she would be ready to come back."

He sighed as the tough memories flooded back. "Eighteen months after she left, she died from a prescription-drug overdose. Doctors said it was probably accidental."

That *probably* always pissed him off. Even the smallest chance that Stephanie might have deliberately chosen to leave the two cutest kids on the planet just about broke his heart.

Something of his emotions must have shown on his

features. Ella made a small sound, her own expression deeply distressed.

"Oh, Beck. I'm so sorry."

"I am, too—for the boys' sake, anyway. They're doing okay, though. They ask about her once in a while, but not so much anymore. They don't remember her. They were only toddlers when she left. They ask after Judy far more often than they do their mother."

"I'm sorry," she said again.

"I don't know why I told you all that," he said. What was it about Ella that compelled him to share details of his life he usually preferred to keep to himself? There was something about her that drew him to her, something more than her pretty eyes and her soft, delicate features.

He liked her. Plain and simple. It had been a long time since he felt these soft, seductive feelings for a woman.

Not that he planned to do a damn thing about it—except spill all his dirty laundry, apparently.

"You're cold. I'm sorry I kept you out here so long."

"I'm not cold," she protested. "Only sad that any woman could deliberately choose to walk away from such amazing boys and—and you."

Was it his imagination or did she blush when she said that? His interest sharpened. Again, he was aware of the tug and pull of attraction between them.

He wanted desperately to kiss her. He ached with it, the hunger to pull her close and brush his lips across hers, gently at first and then, if she didn't push him away, with a little more intensity.

He caught his breath and inclined his head slightly. Her eyes went wide and she swallowed. He thought she might have even leaned toward him, but at the last moment, before he would have taken that chance, the back door opened.

"Hey, what are you still doing out here?" Trevor asked.

He couldn't very well tell his son he was just about to try to steal a kiss. Trevor didn't give him a chance to answer, anyway, before he went on.

"Hey, can Colter and me watch a Christmas show before dinner?" Trevor asked.

After mentally scrambling for a second, Beck did his best to shift back into father mode. It took great effort, especially when all he wanted to do was grab Ella close and explore that delicious-looking mouth until they were both breathless.

He cleared his throat. "You know the rule. The TV can come on when chores are done."

"They are. I just took the garbage out and Colt finished putting away the dishes in the dishwasher."

He couldn't ask for more than that. "Fine. One show. Fair warning, dinner shouldn't take long. You might have to stop the show in the middle, if the food is ready before the show is over."

"Okay." Trevor beamed, then hurried back inside to tell his brother the good news, leaving Beckett along with Ella and this awkwardness that seemed to have suddenly blossomed between them.

"Ella…"

She didn't quite meet his gaze. "Your boys are hungry. We should probably take care of that."

He was hungry, too, but the choice T-bones he had been marinating all afternoon wouldn't slake this particular appetite.

She was right, though. The boys needed to eat—and

he needed to do all he could to regain a little common sense when it came to Ella Baker.

Forty-five minutes later, nerves still shimmied through her from that intense moment on Beck's back step.

Had he really tried to kiss her?

She couldn't be completely sure but was about 95 percent certain. The vibe had certainly been there, crackling through the air between them.

She had done her best to ignore it through dinner, but couldn't seem to stop staring at his mouth at odd, random moments.

She caught herself at it again and jerked her gaze away quickly, setting her napkin beside her plate and leaning back in her chair.

"That was truly delicious," she said, trying for a casual tone. "I'm not exaggerating when I say that was probably the best steak I've ever had. What do you use for a marinade?"

"Nothing too complicated—soy sauce, honey, a little bit of ground black pepper and a splash of olive oil."

"Sometimes the simple things are the best. Thank you again for inviting me to dinner."

"I didn't do anything but grill some steaks and toss a couple of potatoes in the oven to bake. You provided everything else. I should be thanking *you*. Those rolls were little yeasty bites of heaven."

The description pleased her. Why was it so much more fun to cook when people appreciated the effort?

"We're done," Colter announced. "Can we go back and finish our show?"

"Yeah," Trevor chimed in. "The Abominable Snowman guy was just learning how to walk with one foot in front of the other. That's our favorite part."

Ella had to smile, since that had always been her own favorite part of that particular Christmas special.

"Clear your plates first. You can take our guest's, as well, if she's finished."

"I am, thank you."

"Do you want to watch the rest of the show with us?" Trevor asked.

Though the earnestness behind the request touched, Ella glanced at her watch. How had the entire day slipped away?

"Thank you, but it's later than I thought. I should go. I hate to eat and run, but I should probably be home before my father arrives back at the ranch. Sometimes he needs help getting out of his coat and boots."

By the understanding she glimpsed in his gaze, she understood that Beck knew as well as she did that the word *sometimes* was unnecessary. Curt might refuse to admit it, but he *always* needed help. His limitations were growing all the time, something that made her heart hurt whenever she thought about it.

"Let me hurry and wash the salad bowl and the pan you baked the rolls in, so you can take them home clean."

"Unnecessary. I have other dirty dishes at home I still need to wash. I can easily throw these in with them."

He looked as if he wanted to argue but held his tongue.

"Guys," he said instead to his sons, "can you tell Miss Baker thanks for joining us today?"

"Thanks, Miss Baker," they said in unison, something they did often. She wasn't sure they were even aware of it.

"I'm the one who must thank you for the wonderful

day. I'm so grateful to you for sharing your puppies with me and for helping me with my riding lessons again. I owe you. I mean it."

The boys nudged each other, hiding their matching grins that indicated they knew exactly what she meant, that she would in turn help them practice the song for their father before the show the following week.

"You're welcome," Trevor said.

"See you tomorrow. At practice," Colter added, with such a pointed, obvious look, it was a wonder Beckett didn't immediately catch on that something else was going on.

She followed Beck from the dining room to the kitchen. Despite her protests, he ended up washing the pan she had used for the rolls as well as the now-empty salad bowl.

She finally gave up arguing with him about it and picked up a dish towel instead. "While we're at it, we might as well finish cleaning your kitchen. I can spare a few more moments."

This time, he was the one who looked as if he wanted to argue, but after a moment, he shrugged.

She was right, it only took them a few moments. She found the domesticity of the scene dangerously seductive, the two of them working together in the kitchen while the sounds of the Christmas show filtered in from the television that was in a nearby room.

"It really was a great steak," she told him again.

"Thanks. I don't have many specialties in the kitchen, so I'm pretty proud of the few I can claim."

"With reason."

He tossed a spatula in the rinse water and she pulled it out to dry.

"One of the toughest things about us men being on our own now that Judy is gone is figuring out the food thing all the time. She used to leave food in the fridge for us to heat up, but now Jax and Dan and I have to take turns. I think the boys are getting a little tired of burgers and steaks, but that's mostly what I'm good at."

"I hear you. My problem is the opposite. I would like to cook other things, but my dad's a cattleman through and through. Red meat is about all he ever wants, though Manny Guzman's wife prepares meals for us a few times a week and she likes to slip in some chicken dishes here and there."

"You take good care of your father," he said, his voice slightly gruff.

She could feel her cheeks heat at the unexpected praise. "Whether he wants me to or not. He's constantly telling me he doesn't need my help, that I should go back to Boston. That's where my mother lives with her second husband."

"Why don't you?"

She wasn't sure she could articulate all the reasons. "I love my dad. He needs help, no matter what he says, and I'm in a position to offer that help. He doesn't have anyone else. Not really."

She shrugged. "Anyway, I like it here. The people are kind and my job is tremendously rewarding. It hasn't been a sacrifice."

He said nothing, just continued washing the last few dishes, then let the water out of the sink while she wiped down the countertops.

"That should do it," he said when she finished. "Thanks for your help. I've got to say, the kitchen looks better than it has in weeks. None of us enjoys the cleanup portion of the program. That's probably obvious."

"It wasn't bad," she assured him. "You know, even if you don't hire another full-time housekeeper, you could still have someone come in a couple times a week to straighten up for you."

"That would certainly help. Know of anyone looking for a job?"

"Not off the top of my head, but I can ask around." She glanced at the clock on the microwave. "And now I really do have to go. Dad expected he would be home in about a half hour from now. If he makes it home ahead of me, he's going to worry about where I am."

"I'll grab your coat."

He brought it in from the mudroom and helped her into it, which only seemed to heighten her awareness of the heat and that delicious outdoorsy scent that clung to him.

"Thanks again," she said, then reached for her dishes. He beat her to it, picking them up and heading for the door.

"What are you doing?"

"I'll walk you out. Even we Idaho cowboys learn a few manners from our mamas."

"I never said otherwise, did I?"

"No. You didn't," he said gruffly.

Who had? His troubled wife? The thought left her sad.

The storm hadn't started yet. Though it still smelled like impending snow, the clouds had even cleared a little, revealing a few glittery expanses of night sky.

"Oh," she exclaimed, craning her neck. "Look at all those stars. It always takes my breath away."

"Yeah, it's one of the best things about living out here, where we don't have much light pollution."

"A few times when I came here over the summers, my dad would wake me in the middle of the night so we could drive into the mountains to see the meteor shower."

"The Perseids. I do the same thing with the boys. Every August, we take a trail ride up into the hills above the ranch and spread our sleeping bags out under the stars to watch the show."

There was another image that charmed her, the picture of this big, tough cowboy taking his young twin sons camping to show them nature's fireworks show. "That sounds lovely."

"We've got another meteor shower this week. You should check it out."

"Thanks, but I think I'll pass on anything that involves sleeping out under the stars in December."

He smiled as they reached her SUV. She opened the rear door and he slid the pan and bowl inside, then stepped forward to open her door for her.

"Good night," she said. "Thank you again for a lovely afternoon."

"It was my pleasure. The boys loved having you out and…so did I."

His voice was low, intense. Shivers rippled down her spine and she couldn't resist meeting his gaze. All those glittery feelings of earlier seemed to ignite all over again, as if someone had just stirred a hearth full of embers inside her and sent a crackling shower of sparks flaring through her.

They gazed at each other for a long moment and then he uttered a long, heartfelt oath before he lowered his mouth to hers.

Chapter Nine

As his mouth descended and his arms enfolded her against him, Ella caught her breath at the heat and strength of him surrounding her. For a moment, she couldn't think straight and stood frozen in his arms while his mouth brushed over hers once, then twice.

As she blinked in shock, her brain trying to catch up to what was going on, the amazing reality of it seeped in.

She was kissing Beck McKinley—and it was so much better than she ever could have imagined. Still not quite believing this was real, she returned the kiss with all the hunger she had been fighting down for so very long.

She forgot about the boys inside, about the snow spiraling down around them, the cold metal of her SUV seeping through the back of her wool coat.

The only thing she could focus on was Beck—his delicious mouth on hers, the strength of his muscles under her exploring hands, the heat and wonder and sheer thrill of kissing him at last.

She wasn't sure how long he kissed her there in the cold December night—long enough, anyway, that when he pulled away, she felt disoriented, breathless, aware that her entire body pulsed with a low, delicious ache.

"I told myself I wasn't going to do that."

"I… Why?" His words jerked her out of that happy daze.

"Because I was afraid as soon as I kissed you once, I would only want to do it again and again. I was right."

"I wouldn't mind." Some part of her warned her that she probably shouldn't admit that, but the words spilled out before she could stop them.

He gazed down at her, his eyes flashing in the moonlight. He was so gorgeous, rough and masculine. How could any woman resist him?

"I like you, Ella. More than I should."

A thrill shot through her at his words, even though it was tempered by the reluctant way he said them. He liked her, but was obviously not crazy about that fact.

"I like you, too," she admitted. She didn't add that the more time she spent with him, the more she liked him.

Something bright flashed in his gaze and he kissed her again, this time with a fierce intensity that completely took her breath away.

After another moment, he sighed and pulled away, his forehead pressed to hers. "I have to stop, while I still can."

"You don't *have* to."

"It's freezing out here. That snow is going to start in about ten minutes and the temperature will drop more. I have a feeling it might be pretty traumatic for my boys to find us here after the spring thaw, still locked together."

With clear reluctance, he eased away. "That shouldn't have happened, Ella. You get that, right? I can't…start something with you."

Maybe he should have thought of that little fact before he kissed her until she forgot her own name, she thought tartly. After the heated embrace they had just shared, something had already started between them, like it or not.

Oh, this was going to get awkward quickly. She couldn't just ignore the man. They lived in the same community, were neighbors, for heaven's sake. He was at her father's ranch nearly every day for some reason or other.

How was she supposed to be able to look at him in the grocery store or the library or parent-teacher conferences without remembering this moment—the heat of his mouth on hers, the taste of him, minty and delicious.

"You should probably go. Your father will be home soon, if he isn't already."

"Right." Shaky and off balance, she managed to make her limbs cooperate long enough to climb into her driver's seat.

He stood for a moment, looking as if he wanted to say something else, but ultimately he only gave a little wave, closed the door, then stood back so she could drive away.

Her SUV had a key remote that started with a push button. She fumbled with it for several seconds, aware her hands shook and her thoughts were scattered. After an uncomfortably long moment, she somehow remembered she needed to press the brake at the same time she pushed the button before it could start. Finally she managed to combine all the steps and the engine roared to life.

As she drove away, she forced herself not to check the rearview mirror to see if he was still standing there. Her head spun with a jumble of emotions—shock, regret and, most of all, an aching hunger.

He was right. They shouldn't have done that. How on earth was she supposed to go back to treating him with polite distance, when all she would be able to remember was how magical it had felt to be in his arms?

Beck couldn't force himself to move for several moments, even after the taillights of Ella's SUV disappeared down the drive.

What the hell just happened? He felt as if a hurricane had just blown through his world, tossing everything comfortable and familiar into weird, convoluted positions.

Ella Baker.

What was he *thinking*, to kiss her like that?

He had been contemplating the idea of reentering the dating waters for the last year, had even dipped his toe in a bit and asked out a neighbor, Faith Nichols Dustin. That hadn't turned out so well—for him, anyway. Faith was now married to another rancher and friend, Chase Brannon.

He was happy for them. His heart had never really been involved, but he liked Faith and thought they had many things in common. They had both lost their spouses, were raising their children alone, ran successful ranch operations.

On paper, they would have made a good fit. It wasn't to be, though. Faith and Chase were obviously in love, and Beck was happy they'd been able to find joy together after all these years.

He envied them, really. The truth was, he was lonely, pure and simple. His life wasn't empty. Far from it. He had the boys and the ranch, his brother and his uncle, but he missed having a woman in his life. He missed soft skin and sweet smiles, the seductive scent of a woman's warm neck, the protective feeling of sleeping with someone he wanted to watch over in his arms.

He sighed. In the end, it didn't matter how lonely he was. He couldn't make another mistake like Stephanie. He had the boys to worry about now. If he ever became seriously involved with a woman again, he would have to pick someone he absolutely knew would stick—a woman who loved it here as much as he did, who could not only be *content* with the ranching life, but could also embrace it, hardships and all.

Too bad the one woman he had been drawn to in longer than he could remember was someone so completely inappropriate.

Ella Baker was delicate and lovely, yes. He could look at her all day long and never grow tired of it. She made him want to tuck her inside his coat and protect her from the cold, the wind and anything else that might want to hurt her.

She wasn't for him.

He needed a woman from this world, someone tough and hardy and resilient. Someone who wouldn't mind the wind or weather, the relentlessly long hours a rancher had to put in during calving and haying seasons, the self-reliance that was a vital, necessary part of this life.

He couldn't put his boys through losing someone else

they loved, simply because he was drawn to sweet, pretty, delicate types like Ella Baker.

He pressed a hand to his chest, to the sudden ache there. Just a little heartburn, he told himself. It certainly couldn't be something as useless and unwanted as yearning.

His boys were up to something, but damned if Beck could figure out what.

Despite his best and most subtle efforts to probe in the week following that Sunday dinner with Ella, they were being uncharacteristically closemouthed about things.

Still, it was obvious they had secrets. Seemed like they spent half their free time whispering to each other, then going suspiciously quiet whenever he happened to walk in.

He tried to give them a little latitude. It was Christmastime, when everybody seemed to turn into covert operatives, with secrets and hidden stashes of treasure. He had his own secrets right now.

He didn't like that Dan and Jax seemed to be in on the whole thing. More than once, he had seen the boys talking to them, only to shut things off again if Beck walked in.

Knowing something had been stirring at the Broken Arrow all week, he should have been prepared on Friday morning when the boys ganged up and ambushed him at breakfast.

"Dad, can we have Miss Ella over again tomorrow to ride Creampuff?" Trevor asked.

His skin seemed to catch fire just at the mention of her name. The ache in his chest that had been there since their kiss Sunday night seemed to intensify.

He had dreamed about her every single night, but hadn't seen her since then.

"She only rode here two times," Colter reminded him. "That's not enough."

"We promised we would teach her how to ride. If we're gonna do that, it has to be more than two times."

What sort of arrangement had they made with their music teacher? He still couldn't shake the suspicion that there was something fishy about the whole thing from the outset. He thought they were doing a nice thing to invite her out to ride, but he was beginning to wonder if there was something more to it, something he was missing.

What weren't they telling him?

"We thought maybe she could bring us home after practice tomorrow morning and then we can ride in the arena for a while, and then she could go see the new puppies with us," Colter said in what seemed like a deceptively casual tone.

Yes. They were definitely cooking up something.

"And maybe she could stay for dinner again," Trevor suggested blithely. Beck didn't miss the way Colter poked him with his elbow and gave him a shut-up sort of look.

"I don't know about dinner," he said slowly, "but she can certainly come out and ride again, if she wants to. You can invite her at practice. She might be busy, though. It wouldn't surprise me. Everyone seems to be, this time of year."

"We'll ask her," Trevor said. He cast a sidelong look at his brother, who nodded, another of their unspoken twin-talk kind of communications.

"You'll be here tomorrow, won't you?"

"I don't know. Like I said, it's a busy time of year. I'll have to see how my schedule plays out. I have to run into

Idaho Falls at some point this weekend to pick up a few things for Sal and the puppies." And for two certain little caballeros for Christmas, but he didn't tell them that.

"I can always run to Idaho Falls for you." Jax looked up from his coffee and his iPad long enough to make the offer.

"Yeah." Colter seized on that. "Maybe Uncle Jax can go to Idaho Falls for you. It would be better if you could be here when Miss Ella comes over."

"Why's that?" he asked with a frown.

The twins exchanged looks that were not at all subtle. He had seen that look before, too many times to count—usually just moments before they did something dangerous or destructive, like jump from the barn loft or try to take out ornaments on the Christmas tree with their little peashooters.

"Because you're, you know, a really good teacher and good with horses and stuff."

Colter's ready response didn't ease Beck's suspicions any.

"Uncle Jax is a good teacher, too, and he's even better than I am with horses." That wasn't always easy for him to admit, but it was true. His younger brother had an uncanny way with them. "Miss Baker will be okay."

Jax had been watching this exchange with unusual interest. Usually his brother kept to himself until at least his second cup of coffee. "Sure," he answered. "For the record, I'm happy to teach Ella Baker anything she would like to know."

Beck knew he had no right to the giant green tide of jealousy that washed over him at the thought of the sweet Ella in his brother's well-practiced hands.

"We're talking about horses, right?"

Jax gave him an innocent look that didn't fool Beck any more than the boys' had. His brother had the same uncanny way with women that he did with animals.

"Sure. That's what I was talking about. What else would be on my mind?"

Beck could only imagine. His brother was a notorious flirt whose favorite pastime, when he wasn't following the rodeo circuit or training his own horses, was hanging out with buckle bunnies who liked to admire his...trophies.

Come to think of it, he wasn't sure he wanted Jax within half a mile of Ella Baker.

"Maybe she can't even come over," Trevor said. "But we can ask her, right?"

He didn't miss the little thread of yearning in his son's voice. It made him wary and sad at the same time. Since Judy retired, they seemed a little more clingy than usual, probably hungry for a woman's softer arms and gentle ways.

"All you can do is ask. Find out if she's available and then we'll figure out the rest."

"Okay. Thanks, Dad."

"Finish your breakfast and load your dishes. You'd better hustle or you're going to miss the bus."

They shoveled in their eggs, then raced to brush teeth, grab homework and don coats and backpacks. Through it all, they continued to whisper, but he sent them on their way without making any progress at figuring out what secrets they were keeping from him.

Ella did her best to put the memory of that kiss behind her. It should have been easy. She was insanely busy as the calendar ticked inexorably toward Christmas.

In addition to the daily practices for the show at The Christmas Ranch, each of the grades at the elementary school was preparing a small performance for their parents—with plenty of music needed—and her middle school choir presented their annual holiday concert.

She also volunteered at the local senior citizen center in Pine Gulch and had agreed to lead carols for their holiday luncheon.

It was chaotic and hectic and…wonderful. She loved being part of the Pine Gulch community. She loved going to the grocery store and being stopped by at least two or three people who wanted to talk. She loved the way everyone waved as she drove past and gave genuine smiles, as if they were happy to see her.

Though she had good neighbors and friends in Boston, she had never known the same sense of community as she did here in Idaho.

Her life had changed drastically since she came to live with her father the previous year.

Occasionally, she missed her job there, her friends, the active social network and many cultural opportunities she found in Boston. She even missed her mother and stepfather and their lovely home in the Back Bay neighborhood.

She wouldn't go back. Her life here was rich and full and rewarding—even when she found her schedule packed with activities.

She hadn't seen Beck all week, but even her busy routine hadn't kept her from spending entirely too much time thinking about him and about that amazing kiss.

She wasn't sleeping well. Each night she fell into bed, completely exhausted, but her stupid brain seemed to want to replay every moment of that kiss, from the first brush of his mouth on hers to the strength of his muscles against her to the cold air swirling around them.

By the time Friday rolled around, she was completely drained. The show at The Christmas Ranch would be the following Tuesday, which meant only three more rehearsals—that afternoon, Saturday morning and Monday after school. With everything else going on, this would be her last chance to practice with Colter and Trevor for their special number.

Now, as they rehearsed one more time in her classroom, her fingers strummed the last chord of the song and she beamed at the boys.

"That time was perfect!" she exclaimed. "I can't believe how well you've picked up the harmony and you've memorized the words and everything. Your dad is going to love this so much. Everyone else will, too."

She wasn't exaggerating or giving false praise. Colter and Trevor actually sounded so good together, she would have loved to record it.

All her instincts told her that if she ever uploaded it to social media, the song would go viral instantly. Their voices blended perfectly and the twins had a natural harmony that brought out all the emotional punch of the song, the angst of a cowboy who has to spend the holiday alone in the cold elements instead of by a warm fire, surrounded by loved ones.

Beyond that, there was something utterly charming about these two redheaded little boys who looked like the troublemakers many thought they were, but when they opened their mouths, they sang like little cowboy angels.

On the night of the performance, she would have to make sure it was recorded. More than one parent had offered to film the entire show. She would have to be sure

Beck could obtain a copy, especially since he wouldn't be prepared to record it himself, considering the whole thing would be a total surprise.

"Thanks a lot for helping us," Trevor said.

"You're very welcome. I've enjoyed it. And you boys have been so good during the rehearsals. You've more than repaid me."

"No, we haven't," Colter argued. "We still need to take you horseback riding again. You only went two times and we practiced our song almost every day."

"Our dad said we could invite you to come over again tomorrow after practice, if you have time," his brother said.

"Yeah! You've got to come and see the puppies. They're growing *fast*."

"Their eyes are open now and they're not always sleeping every minute. They're so cute. You have to see them," Trevor said. "We got to hold one yesterday. Sal didn't like it much but Dad just petted her and talked to her so she didn't get too mad at us."

"I'm glad to hear that," Ella said, charmed despite herself by the image of Beck giving his boys a chance to hold the puppy.

Only a few weeks ago, she had thought him cold, emotionless. How had she managed to get things so very wrong?

He certainly didn't kiss like he was cold and emotionless. The memory made her ache.

"So do you want to come over after practice tomorrow afternoon?"

With everything on her docket, that was really her only free chunk of time all week to finish her own Christmas preparations, but this appeared to be a matter of honor to the boys. It was clear Trevor and Colter wanted to be sure they repaid her accordingly, after all her work helping them prepare the song.

Beyond that, she felt a little rush of anticipation at the prospect of riding again. She had begun recapturing something she thought had been lost forever and couldn't help being eager to continue on that journey.

"I have a busy day tomorrow, but I think I could make that work. I would love to visit Creampuff again and see Sal and her puppies."

"Yay!" Colter said.

"I'll plan on taking riding clothes again and we can practice after I take you home from rehearsal tomorrow."

"Maybe we can show you how to rope a calf," Colter said.

"I think I'll stick with trying to stay in the saddle," she said with a smile. "Are you sure this is okay with your father?"

Trevor's features fell a little. "He said we could ask you, but he might not be there."

"Yeah. He said he had some stuff to do tomorrow, so our uncle Jax said he could teach you anything you want to know."

"Dad didn't like that very much, though. He was kind of mad at Uncle Jax. He got a big, mean face, but Uncle Jax only laughed."

"Is that right?" she said faintly.

Jax McKinley was a flirt of the highest order. From the moment she moved to town, friends had warned her not to take him too seriously.

"Yeah. Uncle Jax is really good with horses. He even rides broncs in the rodeo and stuff."

"But our dad is even better," Colt assured her. "He's the best cowboy ever."

"And he's nice, too."

"Plus, he can cook good. He makes really good popcorn."

Don't forget that he can kiss like he was born knowing his way around a woman's mouth.

"I'll be grateful to anyone who might be there tomorrow to give me a lesson," she assured them. "Now, we'd better hurry or we'll be late to rehearsal."

As the boys grabbed backpacks and coats and she gathered her own things, she couldn't stop thinking about Beck. Big surprise. What would he think of the boys' special musical number? He would have to possess a heart of lead not to be touched by their effort on his behalf.

They were adorable kids. She would always be grateful she had been able to get to know them a little better these past few weeks.

She had completely changed her perspective about them, too. Somehow they had worked their charming little way into her heart when she wasn't looking.

The trick after the holidays would be figuring out how to extricate them all.

"I thought you were planning to be in Idaho Falls all day."

Beck fought the urge to rearrange that smirk on Jax's too-handsome face. His brother always seemed to know instinctively which buttons to push. Apparently Beck was more transparent than he thought.

"I took care of everything I had to do in town," he said. "It took less time than I expected. I knew what I

wanted and where to get it, so there was no sense daw-
dling, was there?"

"Words to live by, brother." Jax grinned, obviously
taking his words to mean something entirely different
from what Beck intended. "Too bad for me, I guess that
means you can take over the riding lesson with our pretty
little neighbor this afternoon. But I imagine you already
knew that."

Beck frowned at his brother's teasing. "I don't know
what you're talking about," he lied.

Jax only chuckled. "I guess since you're here, you can
do the honors of saddling up all the horses for the lesson.
I suddenly find myself with an afternoon free. Maybe I
should run into town, do a little Christmas shopping."

"Sounds good." He wouldn't mind if his brother decided to stay away all afternoon.

He checked his watch. Practice was supposed to have
ended about fifteen minutes ago, which meant Ella and
the boys should be here shortly.

As unwelcome anticipation churned through him,
Beckett tried to keep himself busy in the horse barn,
readying the horses and the arena for their visitor. He
was mostly unsuccessful, with little focus or direction,
and was almost relieved when he finally heard a vehicle approach.

He set down the leather tack he had been organizing and walked out to greet them, his heart pounding
in his chest.

How had he forgotten how pretty she was? As she
climbed out of her vehicle, winter sunlight glinted on her
hair and her cheeks were rosy and sweet. She wore jeans,
boots and a ranch coat open to reveal another Christmas
sweater. Instantly, he remembered that moment in his

room the week before, when she had appeared there like something out of a dream he hadn't dared remember.

"Hey, Dad," Trevor said, his features lighting up at the sight of them. "I thought you weren't gonna be here!"

"I took care of my business in Idaho Falls faster than I expected," he answered. They didn't need to know that he had practically bought out the entire toy aisle at the big-box store in his rush to get out of there quickly, before the Saturday rush.

"Great!" Colter said. "This way you can give this Ella her lesson."

The two exchanged delighted grins and an uncomfortable suspicion began to take root.

Something was up, all right, and he had a feeling he was beginning to know what that might be. The little troublemakers had romance on their minds. Somehow they must have got it in their heads that he and their music teacher might make a match of it.

Was Jax in on it? What about Dan? Was that the reason Jax was conveniently taking off and that Dan had made a point of saying he had plans today and couldn't help?

Were they all trying to throw him and Ella together?

His cheeks suddenly felt hot as he wondered if that was the whole reason the boys had come up with the idea for these riding lessons.

This wouldn't do. The idea was impossible. Completely out of the question. He didn't have the first idea how to break it to them.

They were children. They only saw a pretty woman who was kind to them, not all the many reasons why a relationship between Ella and Beck could never work.

He suddenly wished he'd stayed in Idaho Falls, so he

could head off this crazy idea before it had any more time to blossom.

Was it too late to drag Jax back to handle the lessons? He still didn't like the idea of his brother here with his flirty smiles and his admiring gaze. Beck would just have to tough it out.

Things would be easier, though, if they didn't stick around here in the intimate confines of the riding arena.

"What do you say we take a quick trail ride up above the house? You can only learn so much while you're riding around in a circle."

"Outside?" Her gaze shifted to the mountains then back to him, her big blue eyes widening.

She had been injured in those mountains, he remembered. He couldn't blame her for being nervous, yet he knew it was a fear she had to overcome if she would ever be able to truly rediscover the joy of riding horses again.

"You'll be okay. We'll keep you safe," he promised. "Do you have warm enough clothing for that?"

"Is anything ever warm enough for the winters around here?"

He had to smile. "Good point. There's no cold like trying to pull a stubborn calf at two in the morning when it's below zero, with a windchill that makes it even colder."

"Brrr."

He looked over her winter gear. "We should have some warmer gloves that will fit you and a snug hat. I would hate to be responsible for you coming down with frostbite."

"You make this whole outing sound so appealing."

Despite her dry tone, he could see the hint of panic in her eyes and in the slight trembling in her hands.

"Don't worry. We won't go far. I've got a fairly well-groomed trail that winds around above the house a little. We can be back in less than an hour. It will be fun, you'll see."

She still didn't look convinced.

"Trust me," he said. "You're never going to love riding a horse again until you let one take you somewhere worth going."

That seemed to resonate with her. She gazed at him, then at the mountains, then finally nodded.

Even if she wasn't for him, the woman had grit. He wanted to tell her so, right there. He wanted to kiss her smack on the lips and tell her she had more gumption than just about anybody he'd ever met.

He couldn't, of course, without giving the boys encouragement that their devious plan was working, so he only smiled and walked back to the barn to bring out the horses.

Chapter Ten

Ella refused to give in to the tendrils of panic coiling through her.

As the boys led out Creampuff and their two horses, saddled and ready to go, she drew in a deep, cleansing breath.

Beck was right. Riding around in an indoor space had been a great introduction for her, but it wasn't much different from a child atop a pony, going around in circles at the county fair. If she truly wanted to get past her fear, she had to take bigger steps, like riding outside, no matter how stressful.

Beck came out leading his own big horse and for a moment, she let herself enjoy the picture of a gorgeous cowboy and his horse in the clear December air.

"Need a boost?" Beck asked as he approached.

She wanted to tell him no, but the placid and friendly

Creampuff suddenly loomed huge and terrifying. "Yes. Thank you," she said.

He helped her into the saddle and gave her thigh a reassuring squeeze that filled her with a complex mix of gratitude and awareness.

"You've got this, El. We'll be with you the whole time."

"Thanks," she mumbled through lips that felt thick and unwieldy.

Beckett mounted his own horse. Ella was again distracted long enough from her worries to wish she didn't have to hold the reins in a death grip so she could pull out her phone and snap his photograph. Her friends back in Boston should have visual proof that she was actually friends with someone who should be featured in men's cologne advertisements.

The Great American Cowboy, at one with his horse and his surroundings.

"Trev, you go in front, then Colt, then Miss Baker," Beck ordered. "I'll bring up the rear. We're just heading up to the springs. You know the way, right, boys? Not too fast, okay? Just an easy walk this time."

"Okay, Dad," Trevor said.

The boys turned their horses and urged them around the ranch house. Creampuff followed the other horses without much direction necessary from Ella as they made their way around the ranch house and toward a narrow trail she could see leading into the foothills.

At first, she was too focused on remaining in the saddle to notice anything else. Gradually, she could feel her muscles begin to relax into the rhythm of the horse. Creampuff really was a gentle animal. She wasn't placid, but she didn't seem at all inclined to any sudden movements or abrupt starts. She responded almost instantly to any commands.

Ella drew in a deep breath scented with pine, snow, leather and horse. It truly was beautiful here. From their vantage point, she could see Beck's ranch, orderly and neat, joining her father's land. Beyond spread the town of Pine Gulch, with the silvery ribbon of the Cold Creek winding through the mountains.

In summer, this would be beautiful, she knew, covered in wildflowers and sagebrush. Now it was a vast, peaceful blanket of snow in every direction.

This was obviously a well-traveled trail and it appeared to have been groomed, as well.

Had he done that for her, so she would be able to take this ride?

Warmth seeped through her at the possibility and she hardly noticed the winter temperature.

Colter turned around in his saddle. "You're doing great," the boy said. "Isn't this fun?"

"Yes," she answered. "It's lovely up here."

Everything seemed more intense—the cold air against her skin, the musical jangle of the tack, the magnificent blue Idaho sky.

After about fifteen or twenty minutes, they reached a clearing where the trail ended at a large round black water tank.

Trevor's horse went straight to the water and the others followed suit.

"This looks like a well-used watering spot."

"Our cattle like to come up here, but if you stuck around long enough, you could also see elk and deer and the occasional mountain lion," Beck said.

"A mountain lion. Oh, my!"

"They're not real scary," Colter assured her. "They leave you alone if you leave them alone."

"We even saw a wolf up here once," Trevor claimed.

"A coyote, anyway," Beck amended.

"I still think it was a wolf, just like the ones we saw in Yellowstone."

"Want to stretch your legs a little before we ride home? We can show you the springs, if you want. There's a little waterfall there that's pretty this time of year, half-frozen."

"Sure."

This time she dismounted on her own and the boys tied the horses' reins to a post there. Beck waded through the snow to blaze a trail about twenty yards past the water tank to a small fenced-off area in the hillside that must be protecting the source of a natural springs from animal contamination. The springs rippled through the snow to a series of small waterfalls that sparkled in the sunlight.

"This is lovely," she murmured. "Do you come up here often?"

"I maintain it year-round. The springs provides most of our water supply on the ranch. We pipe it down from the source but leave some free-flowing. In the winter, this is as far as we can go without cross-country skis or snowshoes. The rest of the year, there's a beautiful back-country trail that will take you to Cold Creek Canyon. It's really a stunning hike or ride."

"Last year, we rode our horses over to see our friend Thomas."

"That sounds lovely."

What an idyllic place for these boys to grow up. Though they had lost their mother so young, they didn't seem to suffer for love and affection. She didn't envy them precisely—how could she, when they didn't have a mother? Still, she wished she could have grown up on the Baker's Dozen with her parents together, instead of having been constantly yanked in opposite directions.

They seemed so comfortable here, confident and happy and loved.

"You should see the wildflowers that grow up here," Beck said as they headed back to the horses. "There's something about the microclimate, I guess, but in the summer this whole hillside is spectacular, with flowers of every color. Lupine and columbine, evening primrose and firewheel. It's beautiful."

"Oh, I would love to see that." She could picture it vividly.

"You're welcome back, anytime," he said. "June is the best time for flowers."

"I'll keep that in mind."

It always amazed her when she went into the back-country around Pine Gulch that all this beauty was just a few moments away. It only took a little effort and exploration to find it.

"Can we go back now?" Colter asked. "I'm kind of cold."

"Yeah. Me, too," his brother said, with a furtive look at the two of them. "You don't have to come with us. You two can stay up here as long as you want. We're okay by ourselves."

Before their father could answer, the boys hopped back on their horses and headed down in the direction they'd come up.

She glanced at Beck, who was watching his sons with a look of consternation.

"Those two little rascals." He shook his head with

an expression that suggested he was both embarrassed and annoyed.

"What was that all about?"

"It's more than a little embarrassing," he admitted. "I think they're up to something. They've been acting oddly all week."

Oh, dear. She hoped the boys didn't reveal their surprise musical number before the performance in a few days.

"I'm sure it's nothing," she said. "Probably just, you know, typical Christmas secrets."

"That's what I thought at first, but not anymore. Today proved it." He was silent for a moment. "I think they're matchmaking."

She stared. "Matchmaking? Us?"

She felt hot suddenly, then cold. Did the boys know she was developing feelings for their father? Had she let something slip?

"I know, it's crazy. I don't have any definite proof, just a vibe I've picked up a time or two. I'm sorry about that."

Was he sorry because he was embarrassed or sorry that his boys might actually be crazy enough to think Ella and he could ever be a match?

"I… It's fine."

"If this keeps up, I'll talk to them. Make sure they know they're way off base."

"It's fine," she said again, though she felt a sharp pang in her heart at his words. "They are right about one thing, though. It is getting cold up here."

"Yeah. Guess we better head down."

"Thank you for showing me the waterfall, for making me ride up here, when I was afraid to try it. It is beautiful."

"You're welcome. Here. Let me help you mount up again."

She wanted to try herself, but her bad leg was aching from the ride and she wasn't sure she could manage it.

He gave her a boost up. This time, though, because of the stiffness in her leg, she faltered a little and his hands ended up on her rear instead of her waist.

Both of them seemed to freeze for just a moment and then he gave a nudge and she was in the saddle.

He cleared his throat. "I swear, I didn't mean to do that."

"I believe you. Don't worry. I guess it's a good thing the boys weren't here to see, right? They might get the wrong idea."

"True enough."

He looked as if he wanted to say something else but finally mounted his own horse. "You go first. I'll be right behind you. Creampuff knows the way."

She drew in a deep breath and headed down the mountainside.

A wise woman would have jumped back in her car and driven away from Beck McKinley and his cute twins the moment she rode back to the barn. Ella was discovering she wasn't very wise, at least not when it came to the McKinley men.

As soon as they arrived back at the horse barn, the twins came out, two adorable little cowboys. "We can put up Creampuff and Ace for you," Colter offered.

Beck looked surprised, then pleased. "That's very responsible of you, boys."

They beamed at the two of them. "While we do that,"

Trevor said, "you can take Miss Ella to see the puppies again."

"She has to see how much they've grown," his brother agreed.

"We'll wait until you're done with the horses, then we can all go see the puppies together."

"We've already seen them this morning, when we had to feed them," Colter reminded him. "And you said it's better if Sal doesn't have that many visitors at once. It stresses her. You said so."

"That's right. I did say that." Above their heads, Beck raised his eyebrows at Ella in a told-you-so kind of look.

"Go on, Dad. We promised Miss Baker she could see them."

"I guess I have my orders," he murmured to Ella. "Shall we?"

She didn't see a graceful way out of the situation, so she shrugged and followed him toward the older barn.

"What did I tell you?" Beck said as they headed inside from the cold December afternoon to the warm, cozy building.

"You might be right," she said.

"I'm sorry. I don't know what's come over them."

"You don't need to apologize. I think it's rather sweet. I'm flattered, if you want the truth, that they think I'm good enough for you."

You *obviously don't, but it's nice that your sons do.*

He gazed at her for a moment, before shaking his head. "They're rascals. I'll have a talk with them."

Though she fought the urge to tell him not to do that, at least until after Christmas, she knew he had to set them straight. Nothing would ever happen between her and Beck. He had made that abundantly clear.

They stood just inside the door of the barn. It was warm here and strangely intimate and she had to fight the urge to step forward and kiss away that rather embarrassed expression.

He was gazing at her mouth, she realized, and she saw awareness flickering there in his eyes.

He wanted to kiss her and she ached to let him.

No. That wouldn't do, especially if they wanted to convince the boys there was nothing between them.

She curled her hands into fists instead. "We'd better take a look at the puppies, since that's the reason we came in here."

After an awkward moment, he shrugged. "You're right. Absolutely right."

He turned and headed farther into the barn and she followed him to the stall that housed Sal and her new little brood.

Holding on to her suddenly grim mood was tough in the presence of the eight adorable little black-and-white puppies, who were now beginning to toddle around the stall. They appeared less rodentlike and more like cute puppies, furry and adorable, with paws and ears that seemed too big for their little bodies.

"The boys were right!" she exclaimed. "They've grown so much since I saw them last."

"You can hold one, if you'd like. Sal can be a bit territorial so I'll have to grab one and bring it out to you."

"I'm all right. I'll just watch this time."

"Come back in a few weeks and they'll be climbing all over. She'll be glad to let someone else entertain them for a moment."

"They're really beautiful, Beck."

He gazed down at her with a slight smile and she was

aware of the heat of him and the breadth of his shoulders. She felt a long, slow tug in her chest, as if invisible cords were pulling her closer to him.

"Thank you for sharing them with me—and for the rest of today. I'm glad you made me go on that trail, even though it scared me to death."

"I could tell."

She made a face. "Was I that obvious? I thought I was doing so well at concealing my panic attacks"

"There was nothing overt, just a few signs I picked up." He paused. "I hope you realize there's nothing wrong with being afraid, especially after your experience in childhood. Anyone would be. But not everyone would have the courage to try to overcome it."

"I don't think it's *wrong*, necessarily. Only *frustrating*. I don't want to be afraid."

"But you did it anyway. That's the important thing. You've got grit, El. Pure grit."

His words slid around and through her, warming her as clearly as if he'd bundled her in a soft, sweet-smelling quilt just off the clothesline. "I do believe that's the sweetest thing you've ever said to me."

He scratched his cheek, looking sheepish. "It must be the puppies. They bring out my gooey side."

"I like it," she confessed.

As he looked down at her, she again felt that tug in her chest, as if everything inside her wanted to pull her toward him. He must have felt it, too. She watched his expression shift, saw the heat spark to life there. His gaze slid to her mouth then back to meet her gaze and he swallowed hard.

Sunlight slanted in through a high window, making his gorgeous features glow, as if the universe was somehow telling her this was right. She had never been so aware of a man. He could carry her over his shoulders to one of the straw-covered stalls and she wouldn't utter a peep of protest.

The air around them seemed to hiss and snap with a sweet, fine-edged tension, and when he sighed and finally kissed her, it seemed as inevitable as a brilliant summer sunset.

Kissing him felt as familiar and *right* as being on a horse had earlier that afternoon. His mouth fit hers perfectly and he wrapped his arms around her as if he had been waiting for just this moment.

She returned his kiss eagerly, with all the pent-up longing of the previous week, when she had been tormented by heated memories.

Through the thrill and wonder of the kiss, as his mouth explored hers and his hands somehow found their way beneath her sweater to the bare skin of her lower back, she was aware of a tiny, ominous thread weaving through the moment.

It took several more long, delicious kisses before she could manage to identify the source of that little niggling worry, the grim truth she had been trying to ignore.

This was more than simple attraction.

She was falling in love with Beckett McKinley.

The realization seemed to knock the air right out of her lungs and she was suddenly more afraid than she'd been the first time she faced his horses.

He would hurt her. Badly. Oh, he wouldn't mean to— Beck was a good man, a kind one, as she had figured out over the last little while. But he had no real use for her beyond a few kisses. He had made that perfectly clear—

as far as Beck was concerned, she didn't belong here. She was no different from his late wife or her own mother.

Like her father, he couldn't see the truth of her, the part that loved afternoon thundershowers over the mountains or the sight of new crops breaking through the ground or a vast hillside covered in wildflowers.

One of the puppies made a little mewling whimper that perfectly echoed how she felt inside. Somehow it gave Ella the strength to slide her mouth away from his.

She caught her breath and tried to make light of the kiss, purely in self-defense. "Good thing your sons didn't come in just now. If they had seen us wrapped together there, they might have made the mistake of thinking we're both falling in exactly with their plans."

"Good thing," he murmured, looking dazed and aroused and gorgeous.

She had to get out of here, before she did something stupid, like yank him against her again and lose her heart the rest of the way. She drew a deep gulp of air into her lungs and forced a casual smile that she was fairly sure didn't fool him for a moment.

"I should, um, go. I've got a Christmas party tonight with some friends and still have to bake a dozen cookies for the exchange."

He said nothing for a long moment, then sighed. "Should we talk about that?"

She opted to deliberately misunderstand. "The cookies? I'm making my favorite white-chocolate cranberry recipe. There's really nothing to it. The secret is using a high-quality shortening and a little more flour, especially in this altitude."

"I'm sure you know I didn't mean we should talk about

the cookies—though those sound delicious. I meant the kiss."

He shoved his hands into the pockets of his coat, as if he was afraid if he didn't, he would reach for her again.

Or maybe his fingers were simply cold.

"There's nothing to say," she said with that fake smile that made her cheek muscles hurt. "The boys can play matchmaker all they like, but we both know it won't go anywhere. I'll just make a point not to visit any cute puppies alone with you again."

While she was at it, she would have to add walking together to her car to that list of no-no's, as well as helping her onto a horse and washing dishes side by side.

Come to think of it, maybe it would be better if they kept a nice, safe, ten-foot perimeter between them at all times.

"I really do have to go," she lied.

"I guess I'll see you next week at the Christmas show."

She nodded and hurried out before she did something else stupid.

Beck followed her out to be sure she made it safely to her vehicle. There were a few icy spots that worried him, but she hurried across the yard to her SUV and climbed inside without faltering or looking back, as if one of his cow dogs was nipping at her heels to drive her on.

He had screwed up. Plain and simple.

For nearly a week, he'd been telling himself all the reasons he couldn't kiss her again. What did he do the first moment they were really alone together? Yep. He kissed her. He hadn't been able to help himself. She had been so soft and sweet and lovely and all he could think about was tasting her mouth one more time.

The trouble was, he was not only fiercely attracted to her, but he also genuinely liked her.

He meant what he said to her. She had more grit than just about anybody he knew.

If she had the kind of raw courage necessary to ride again after an accident that nearly killed her, why was he so certain she didn't belong out there, that she would turn tail and run at the first sign of trouble?

She wasn't like Stephanie. That was clear enough. Yes, they had both been raised back east in big cities. They both came from wealthy, cultured backgrounds that seemed worlds away from this small Idaho town.

But Stephanie had been...*damaged*. He should have seen that from the start. She had managed to hide it fairly well at first, but when he looked back, he could clearly see all the warning signs he should have discerned much earlier. He hadn't *wanted* to see them. He had been busy growing the ranch, getting ready for the arrival of his sons, coping with a moody, temperamental wife.

If he had been more aware, maybe he could have found help for her earlier and headed off the debilitating depression that came later.

The truth was, he didn't trust himself these days. Things had gone so horribly wrong with Stephanie, and his sons had been the ones to suffer. He couldn't afford to mess up again.

If he didn't have the boys to consider—only himself— he might take the chance to see if these tender young feelings uncurling inside him for Ella Baker could grow into something sturdy and beautiful.

How could he take that risk, though?

If he pursued things between them and she ended up

leaving, too, like their mother—and like her own, for that matter—the boys would be shattered.

He couldn't do that to them.

He turned around and headed back to the barn, aware as he walked that Ella had the strength to confront her fears while he was letting his own completely chase him down and wear him out like one of the Yellowstone wolves on a wounded calf.

Chapter Eleven

If he could have avoided it, Beck would have stayed far away from the Baker ranch until he could manage to figure out a way to purge Ella out of his system.

He had a feeling he faced a long battle on that particular front.

Meanwhile, he couldn't avoid the place, especially not while he and Curt were still the copresidents of the local cattle growers association.

They had end-of-year paperwork to finish for the association. It had been on his desk for a week, but he had been putting it off. Finally, the day of the Christmas show the boys had been working so hard on, he knew he couldn't put it off any longer.

It was no coincidence that he tried to time his visit around noon, as he was certain Ella would be busy teaching music at the school and not here to torment him with visions of what could never be.

If that made him a yellow-bellied chicken, he would just have to live with it.

"Thanks for bringing this by," Curt said, gesturing to the folder of papers he needed to sign.

"No problem. I was out anyway," Beck assured him. "I'm heading over to Driggs to pick up the last thing for the boys' Christmas. I commissioned new saddles for each of them, since they're growing so fast and are too big for the ones they've been using."

"Watch those two. They'll be taller than you before you know it."

Since he was six-two and the boys were only seven years old, Beckett was pretty sure he was safe for a few more years on that front, unless they had an explosive growth spur.

"Need anything while I'm out?"

Curt shook his head and Beck couldn't help thinking his friend looked more frail every time he saw him.

"I can't think of anything," he said. "I did most of my shopping online this year, since it's hard for me to get around the crowded stores."

"Got it."

Curt gazed out the window, where a light snow had begun to fall in the last hour. "It's not coming down too much, but you'd still better hurry back from town. We've got a big storm heading this way."

"That's what I heard."

The weather forecast was predicting the storm might break records.

"It's not supposed to hit until tonight, but you never know. Better safe than sorry. I know you would hate to miss the show tonight at The Christmas Ranch."

"I'll be back in plenty of time. I'm only making one stop to the saddle maker's place."

"Good. Good." Curt reached for the big water bottle on the table beside him but his hands were trembling so badly today that it took him three tries to find the straw.

"How are you doing?" Beck asked. "Really doing?"

It seemed as if they always talked *around* Curt's condition and the challenge it presented, instead of talking *about* it. The older man frowned. For once, he didn't give his stock answer.

"I can't do a damn thing anymore," he said, frustration vying with self-pity in his voice and expression.

"I'm sorry," Beck said, though the words were hardly adequate.

"Parkinson's is the worst. I can barely sign my damn name on those papers. You saw me. If I could climb up on a horse right now, I would borrow one from you. He and I would ride up into the backcountry to die and you'd never see me again."

Man, it was hard to see such an independent, strong man laid low by this debilitating disease.

"That would be a waste of a good horse. Not to mention a good friend," he said quietly.

Curt sipped at his water again, then set it down on the desk in his ranch office. "Have you thought more about buying me out?"

There it was. The other thing he didn't know what to do about.

"Sure I've thought about it. I've run the numbers dozens of times. It's an amazing offer, Curt. I would love the chance to combine our two ranches and build the Baker-McKinley brand into one of the strongest in the world."

"You sound hesitant, though. Is it the asking price? We can negotiate a little."

He could handle the hefty price tag Curt was asking. It would mean leveraging his capital, but he'd had some great years and had money in the bank. What better use for it than taking advantage of the chance to double his usable acreage and water supply, not to mention keeping the Baker's Dozen land out of the hands of developers?

Like everywhere else in the West, this part of Idaho was experiencing a population boom, with people wanting to relocate here for the beautiful views, serenity and slower pace.

As developers built houses and newcomers moved in, they tended to crowd any agricultural operations farther and farther to the outskirts. It was the eternal paradox. People moved to an area because they loved the quiet way of life and what it represented, then immediately set out to change it.

"It's not the price," he said.

"Then what?" Curt persisted. "I'd like to seal this deal as soon as we can."

"What about Ella?" he asked, finally voicing the one concern that seemed to override all the others.

"What about her?"

"How does she feel about you selling the ranch to me?"

Curt flicked off the question with a dismissive gesture. It was obvious from his expression that he didn't consider that an obstacle at all. "She'll be fine with it. It's not like I'm *giving* it to you out of the goodness of my heart, right?"

True enough. He would pay a hefty sum, even slightly above market value.

"Ella stands to inherit my entire estate," Curt went on. "She's all I've got, so the whole kit and caboodle goes to her. Believe me, she's not stupid. She'll be better off having cold hard cash in the bank than being saddled with a cattle ranch she doesn't know the first thing to do with."

The words were barely out of the other man's mouth when Beck heard a gasp from the hallway outside the office.

With a sinking heart, he shifted his gaze and found Ella standing there, holding a tray that looked like it contained a bowl of soup and a sandwich for her father.

The tray wobbled in her hands and he thought for a moment she would drop it, but she righted it at the last moment. She didn't come inside, simply stood there looking devastated.

"Dad," she whispered.

Curt had the grace to look embarrassed. "How long have you been home?"

She ignored the question. "You're selling the ranch? To *Beck*?"

She said his name like it was a vile curse word and he flinched a little. None of this was his idea but he still felt guilty he had even discussed it with Curt.

"I offered it to him. We're still working out terms, but it makes the most sense for everyone."

She aimed a wounded look at Beck, which made him feel sandwiched between father and daughter. "You never said a word to me," she said to him.

He should have mentioned it. Now he wished he had, especially after the first time they kissed.

"Why didn't you tell me?"

Guilt pinched at him, harsh and mean. On its heels, though, was defensiveness. *He* had nothing to feel guilty about, other than not telling her Curt had approached him with an offer to sell. It hadn't been his idea or anything he had deliberately sought out. He had assumed her father had already told her about it.

Anyway, Curt was right. She would inherit the proceeds from the ranch and could live comfortably the rest of her life.

"It makes the most sense for everyone—" he began.

"Not for me! I love this ranch. I'd like to try running it, if my stubborn father would ever let me. I'm trying to learn everything I can. Why do you think I wanted the boys to teach me how to ride?"

"Ride what? I hope you're not talking about horses," Curt interjected, color suffusing his features.

"I am," Ella declared as she finally moved into the room and set down the lunch tray on the desk. "I've been to the Broken Arrow several times to go riding with Trevor and Colter."

"I can't believe you went horseback riding without telling me!"

"Really?" she snapped. "That's what you're taking out of this discussion? Considering you've all but sold my legacy out from under me without bothering to mention it, I don't think you've got much room to be angry about me riding a horse a few times."

"It's not your legacy until I'm gone," her father snapped back. "Until then, I've got every right to do what I want with *my* ranch."

The color that had started to rise on her features leached away and she seemed to sway. Beck half rose to catch her but earned only a scathing glare for his efforts.

"You certainly would never consider trusting me with it, would you?"

"You have no idea how hard this life is."

"Because you've shielded me from it my entire life!"

"For your own good!"

Now she was trembling, he saw, just as much as she had when facing down her fears and riding a horse.

"I'm twenty-seven years old, Dad. I'm not a broken little girl in a hospital bed. I'm not some fragile flower, either. I'm tough enough to handle running the Baker's Dozen. Why can't you see that?"

Curt's jaw clenched. "You have other talents, honey. You don't need to wear yourself out on this ranch."

"What if I want to? I love it here. You know I do."

"You love it *now*. Who's to say that won't change in a week or month or year from now? You have lived on the Baker's Dozen maybe a total of two years your entire life. I just don't want you to be saddled with more than you can handle."

"That's my decision to make, isn't it?"

"No," he said bluntly. "Beckett can take what I've built over my whole life—and what my father's built and his father—and make it even better. Can you say the same?"

She said nothing, only pressed her lips together. Her eyes looked haunted now, hollow with shadows.

Curt appeared oblivious to her reaction. He shrugged. "I wouldn't sell the ranch to Beck just to hurt you, honey. You know that, right?"

"But it *would* hurt me," she answered. "What hurts me more is that you will never even give me the chance to try."

She took a deep breath, as if fighting for control, then turned toward the door. "I can't do this right now. Not today. We can talk about it later. Right now, I have to go back to take my afternoon classes then focus on the children's Christmas show. I'll take the things I need for the show tonight. Don't expect me home between school and the performance."

She left without looking again at either of them, leaving behind an awkward, heavy silence.

Curt winced and picked up his water bottle again in hands that seemed to be shaking more than they had earlier. "I didn't want her finding out about our deal like that."

Beck frowned. "We don't have a deal. Not yet."

He was angry suddenly that Curt had dragged him into the middle of things and felt terrible for his part in hurting her. "If Ella wants to try running the ranch, Curt, I don't think I can stand in the way of that."

"She might think she wants it but she has no idea what it takes to keep this place going. She's never had to pull a calf when it's thirty below zero outside, or be up for forty-eight hours straight, trying to bring the hay in on time."

"So she can hire people to help her. You're not doing it on your own, either. Your foreman has stepped up to take on more and more of the load over the last few years. Why can't he do the same for her?"

"It's not the same. I know what I'm doing! I'm still involved in the day-to-day operations. What does Ella know about cattle? She can play four instruments and sings like a dream but she's not a rancher!"

"Not if you don't let her learn, Curt. Why are you trying so hard to protect her?"

"This ranch almost killed her once. I can't let it finish the job."

Curt blurted out the words, then looked as if he wished he could call them back.

Beck sat back, understanding dawning. He had suspected something like that after Ella told him about her accident.

"Your daughter inherited more from you than your eye color, Curtis Baker. She's tougher than you give her credit. You should have seen the grit she used to get back in the saddle, when it was obvious it scared her to death."

"I can't lose her," the man said, his voice low. "She's all I have."

"If you keep treating her like she's incompetent, you might not have much choice," he answered firmly. "You'll lose her anyway."

Ella sat in her SUV at the end of the driveway, trying to control the tears that burned her eyes.

No good deed goes unpunished, right? She thought it would be a nice thing to surprise her dad for lunch by bringing home a sandwich and some of his favorite take-out tomato bisque from the diner in town.

She never expected she would find Beck in her father's office, or walk in on the two of them negotiating away her future.

Her father had no faith in her.

She had suspected as much, but there was something heartbreaking and final about hearing it spoken so bluntly.

She'll be better off having cold hard cash in the bank than being saddled with a cattle ranch she doesn't know the first thing to do with.

Since coming to live here, she had done her best to learn the ropes. When she wasn't teaching music, she had helped with the roundup, she had driven the tractor, she had gone out with Manny to fix fences.

It wasn't enough. It would never be enough. Curtis Baker could never see her as anything more than a weak, frightened girl.

Did she know everything about running a ranch? No. But she was willing to learn. Why wouldn't her father let her try?

She brushed away a tear that fell, despite her best efforts.

She was stuck here. Her father needed her help. She couldn't just abandon him. But how could she face living here day after day with the knowledge that the ranch she loved—the ranch that felt like a huge part of her—would someday belong to someone else?

To Beck?

The pain intensified, bringing along the bitter taste of betrayal. Damn him. Why hadn't he bothered to mention that Curt had approached him about buying the ranch?

That hurt almost as much as her father's disregard for her feelings.

She let out a breath and swiped at another tear. Just as she dropped her hand, a knock on the window of her vehicle made her jump halfway out of her seat.

She turned to find Beck, big and rugged and gorgeous, standing out in the gently falling snow.

She thought about putting her SUV in gear and spraying him with mud as she peeled out, but that would be childish.

Wouldn't it?

He gestured for her to roll down her window. After a moment, she did but only about three inches. Cold air rushed in, heavy with the impending storm.

"I don't have time to talk to you," she snapped. "I have a class in twenty minutes."

"The school is only a ten-minute drive from here. That means we still have ten minutes."

She set her jaw. Did he think she could just run into her classroom and miraculously be in a mental space to take on thirty-three fourth graders who had been dreaming of sugarplums for weeks?

"What do you want?" she said. Even as she spoke, she was aware she sounded like one of those fourth graders having a verbal altercation with a schoolmate.

"I'm sorry I didn't tell you your father had offered to sell me the ranch. I guess I assumed you and Curt had already talked about it. I thought maybe that was the reason you're sometimes a little...cool to me."

Had she been cool to him? She was remembering a few specific encounters when the temperature had been the exact opposite of cool.

"He never said a word to me. But why would he? As he made it abundantly clear in there, he doesn't need to tell me anything."

Beck sighed. "He should have. Told you, I mean. That's what I just said to him. More than that, I think he should give you a chance to run the Baker's Dozen along with him for a few years, then both of you can decide if you want to sell."

"That's a lovely idea. He would never consider it."

"Have you talked to him about it?"

"Of course! Dozens of times. My father sees what he wants to see. Like I said in there, to him, I'll always be that broken girl in a hospital bed."

"He loves you and worries about you. Speaking as a father, it would be hell to see your child hurt and spend all these years afraid it was your fault."

Curt had sold all his horses after her accident, though he had always loved to ride.

She sighed. "I can't worry about this today," she said. "In a few hours, I'm in charge of a show that involves dozens of children, twenty songs and an audience of three hundred people. I don't have time to stress about my stubborn father right now."

Tomorrow she would. Tomorrow her heart would probably break in jagged little pieces. She would compartmentalize that for now and worry about it after the show. The children had worked too hard for their music director to fall apart because her father had no faith in her.

"I'm sorry," he said again.

"I'm sure you are. Not sorry enough that you would refuse to buy the ranch, though, are you?"

A muscle worked in his jaw but he didn't answer. His silence told her everything she needed to know.

"That's what I thought. I have to go. Goodbye, Beckett."

She put her SUV in gear and pulled out into the driveway, her heart aching with regret and sadness and the tantalizing dream of what might have been.

Chapter Twelve

"Okay, kids. This is it. Our audience is starting to arrive. You've practiced so hard, each one of you. I hope you know how proud of you I am. Each number sounds wonderful and I know you've all put in so much effort to memorize your parts and the words to the music. This show is going to be amazing! Let's make some people happy!"

The children cheered with nervous energy and she smiled reassuringly at them all, though she could feel emotion building in her throat.

This was her second year directing the Christmas show and it might just be her last. If her father sold the ranch to Beckett, she wasn't sure she could stay in Pine Gulch, as much as she loved it here. It would be too difficult to watch.

She snared her thoughts before they could wander

further down that path. Tonight wasn't about sadness and regret, but about the joy and wonder and magic of Christmas. For the children's sake, she needed to focus on the show right now. She would have time to process the pain and disappointment of the day later, when this program was behind her.

"Our guests are arriving now but they will need to eat dinner first. That gives us about thirty minutes before our show. Everyone follow the older girls into the office. We have a special treat in store for you. Celeste Delaney is going to read to you from the newest, still-unpublished Sparkle the Reindeer book!"

An electric buzz crackled through the crowd at that announcement. She knew the children would be excited about the prospect of a new Sparkle book, as everyone adored the charming stories.

When she was certain the children were settled comfortably, Ella returned to the large reception room in the lodge to check on the rapidly filling tables. She greeted a few friends and made small talk as she assessed the crowd.

"We crammed in three more tables, so fifty more people can squeeze in." Hope Santiago came to stand beside her and watch people jostling for space. "I hated to turn people away last year. I hope we've got enough room this year."

It still might be tight, judging by the crowds still coming in.

"How's the weather?" she asked. It wasn't a casual question.

Hope shrugged. "It's snowing a bit but it's not too bad, yet. I still enlisted everybody with four-wheel drive to pick up some of the senior citizens who don't like to drive in the snow. I was hoping we wouldn't have to do that again this year but Mother Nature didn't cooperate. Thanks for signing up Beck, by the way. He's out there now, bringing in his last shuttle group."

So much for trying not to think about the man. She couldn't seem to escape him.

"The show is amazing, El," Hope said, her expression earnest. "You've outdone yourself this year. Every number is perfect. Honestly, I don't know what we would do without you."

She wasn't yet ready to tell her friend The Christmas Ranch might have to do just that next year.

Instead, she forced a smile and prepared to go back and check on the children. To her shock, she came face-to-face with her father, who was just coming in from outside.

What was he doing there? Curtis hadn't said a word to her earlier about attending the show.

An instant later, Beck came in behind him, helping a woman whose name she didn't know navigate the crowd with a walker.

Beck must have given her father a ride. Big surprise. The two of them were no doubt plotting their ranching world domination.

That wasn't really fair, she acknowledged, a little ashamed of herself. Her father and Beck had been friends and neighbors a long time.

Beck looked up from helping the woman and caught sight of her. Something flashed in his gaze, something intense and unreadable.

She let out a breath. Despite her hurt over that scene in her father's office that afternoon, she couldn't help a little shiver of anticipation.

He was going to love the special number his twins had prepared for him out of sheer love. She had no doubt it would touch everyone at the performance—especially Beck.

In a small way, she felt as if the gift was coming from her, as well.

She turned away just as Hope hurried over to her. "We've got a little problem. Somehow two of the angels showed up without their wings. There's no time for someone to fetch them. I know we had extras. Do you remember where we put them?"

"Absolutely. I can picture the box in the storage room perfectly. I'll grab them." She hurried away, forcing herself again to focus on the show and not on her impending heartbreak.

"Oh, Ella. This show has been nothing short of magnificent this year," Celeste whispered backstage as a trio of girls, including her stepdaughter, Olivia, bowed to thunderous applause out on stage. "We could stop there and it would be absolutely perfect. Well done!"

She smiled at her friend. She had to agree. So far the show had gone off without a hitch.

"Is it time for us to go out for 'Silent Night'?" one of the older girls asked.

"In a moment. We have one more special number."

None of the other volunteers or the children in the program had heard Colter and Trevor's song yet, as she and the twins had practiced in secret. Only Hope knew about it, since Ella had to work out the lighting and sound with her and Rafe.

"After we're done, I need you girls to lead the younger

children out, then we'll sing the final number. Boys, are you ready?"

Trevor and Colter both nodded, though their features were pale in the dim light backstage. She had a feeling they would look nervous under any light conditions, as if only now realizing the magnitude of what they had signed up for that long-ago day when they had approached her about singing in the show.

She picked up her guitar from the stand and walked out ahead of the boys, who looked absolutely adorable in matching white shirts with bolo ties and Christmas-patterned vests that Hope had sewn for them. They wore matching cowboy hats and boots and giant belt buckles that were just about as big as their faces.

Oh, she hoped Rafe was videoing this.

Ella sat on a stool as the boys took to the microphone. The crowd quieted, all the restless stirring and rustling fading away.

She had performed enough times to know when she had an audience's attention. With the spotlights on her, it was tough to see Beckett's reaction, but she thought she saw his eyes widen. He would no doubt be completely shocked to see his sons up here onstage, since he had no idea they were performing a duet.

Ella didn't want this number to be about her, but she felt compelled to take the microphone before the boys began.

"It is my great pleasure to introduce to you Colter and Trevor McKinley. They're seven years old. And yes, you guessed it, they're twins."

This earned a ripple of laughter, since that was more than obvious to anyone without cataracts.

Ella waited for the reaction to fade away before

she went on. "A few weeks ago, Trevor and Colter approached me with a rather unusual request. They wanted to perform a special song at this Christmas show as a gift to someone they love very much. They asked me to help them prepare, so it would be perfect. Since then, they have been practicing several times a week with me after school, trying to learn the harmony, the pitch, the dynamics."

She smiled at the boys. "They have worked very hard, which I see as a testament to the value of this gift, which is intended for one person—their father, Beckett."

Though she was a little afraid to look at him, her gaze seemed to unerringly go in his direction. In the brief instant their gazes met, she saw complete shock on his features as people around him smiled and patted him on the back.

"This is his favorite Christmas song, apparently," she went on, "and I have it on good authority he sings it to himself when no one is around."

She didn't look at him now, but she was quite certain he would be embarrassed at that snippet of information. Too bad for him.

"While Trevor and Colter prepared this song especially for their father," she continued, "this is one of those rare and wonderful gifts that benefits more than its recipient. We all are lucky enough to be able to enjoy it. Boys."

She leaned back and softly strummed the opening chords on her guitar. For just a moment, the boys stood frozen in the spotlight, missing their cue by about a half second, but Trevor nudged his brother and a moment later, their sweet young voices blended perfectly as they sang the slow, pensive opening bars.

The crowd seemed hypnotized while the boys sang about spending Christmas Eve in the saddle, about feeling alone and unloved, about finding the true meaning of Christmas while helping the animals.

They had never sung the song so beautifully or with such stirring emotion. When they finished, even Ella—who had heard them sing it dozens upon dozens of times—had to wipe away a tear.

After the last note faded, the crowd erupted into thunderous applause.

"You did great," she murmured over the noise of the crowd. The boys beamed and hugged her, which made more tears slip out.

"Thank you for playing your guitar and teaching us the song," Trevor said solemnly over the noise of the crowd.

Oh, she would miss these sweet boys. She wasn't sure how her heart would bear it.

"You're very welcome," she said. "Now, go find your places for the final song."

The boys rushed to their designated spots as the other children surged onto the stage—angels and shepherds, candy canes and cowboys and ballet dancers in tutus. It was a strange mishmash of costumes, but somehow it all worked perfectly together.

Olivia, who had a pure, magical voice and performed professionally, took the guitar from Ella as they had arranged, and stepped forward to strum a chord. She sang the first line of the song, then the other children joined her to sing "Silent Night" with a soft harmony that rose to fill the St. Nicholas Lodge with sweet, melodious notes.

On the last verse, the senior citizens were encouraged to sing along, which they did with stirring joy.

When the last note died away and the audience again erupted in applause, Hope went to the microphone, wiping away a few of her own tears.

"If you're all not overflowing with Christmas spirit now, I'm afraid there's no hope for you," she declared stoutly, which earned appreciative laughter.

"Wasn't that a spectacular show?" Hope asked.

She had to wait for the audience to quiet before she could speak again. "So many people had a hand in bringing this to you. The fabulous caterer, Jenna McRaven, the high school students who volunteered to serve the meal to you, those who provided the transportation."

She paused and smiled at Ella. "I would especially like to thank the one person without whom none of this would have happened tonight. Our director, organizer, producer and general talent-wrangler, Miss Ella Baker."

The crowd applauded her and she managed a smile. These were her friends and neighbors. They had embraced her, welcomed her in their midst. How would she be able to say goodbye to them?

"Now, I do have a rather grave announcement," Hope went on. Her tone was serious enough that the crowd quieted again and fixed attention on her. "While we were here enjoying this fantastic dinner and truly memorable entertainment, Mother Nature decided to let loose on our little corner of paradise outside with a vengeance. I guess she was mad she wasn't invited to the show so decided to put on her own. As much as I know we all love to visit with each other, I'm afraid that's not a good idea tonight. There will be other chances. We're going to cut things short now and encourage you all to head for home as soon as you can, before conditions get even worse— though if all else fails, we can hitch up the reindeer and sleigh to carry you home. Safe travels to you all, friends. Good night and merry Christmas."

The audience applauded one last time and gave the children a standing ovation, then people began to gather up their coats and bags and stream toward the door.

For the next several moments, Ella tried to hug as many of the children as she could and thank them for their hard work. Through it all, she noticed The Christmas Ranch staff quietly ushering people out.

"I'm sensing urgency here," she said when her path intersected with Hope's through the crowd. "Is it really that bad?"

Hope's eyes were shadowed. "I've never seen a storm come on so quickly," she admitted. "We've already got a foot of new snow and the wind out there is howling like crazy. If the crowd wasn't so noisy in here, you would hear it rattling the windows. I want people to hurry home, but I don't want to incite a panic. It's going to take some time to get everyone out of here."

"I can take more than one group." Somehow, Beckett had appeared at her side without warning and she jumped. She told herself it was only surprise, but she suspected it was more nerves. She was dying to ask how he enjoyed the song, but the urgency of the storm evacuation took precedence.

"Thanks, Beckett. I knew there was a reason I adored you." Hope smiled at him so widely that Ella might have felt a twinge of jealousy if she didn't know Hope adored her husband, Rafe.

"I'll have to factor in taking the boys, too. I'll drop them off in the first batch, then come back for a second trip."

"I can take my father home, so you don't have to do

that," Ella said, though she was still so angry with her father, she didn't know if she could be in the same vehicle with him. "If you want, I can also drop the boys off at the Broken Arrow, as it's on our way home. That should free up a couple more spots in your truck for people who need rides home."

He looked torn. "That's true, but I would feel better if you could head straight home, instead of having to detour to our place."

"We'll be fine," she said. She couldn't believe the storm was really that bad. "I have four-wheel drive and new snow tires. I'm not worried."

One of The Christmas Ranch workers came up to ask Hope a question and she walked away to deal with the situation. When they were gone, Beck turned to her, his expression solemn.

"El, I... Thank you for helping the boys with that song. I've never been so touched. It means more than I can ever say."

Warmth seeped through her at the intensity in his voice. "They did all the hard work. I only guided them a little," she said. "Anyway, we made a fair trade. They agreed to give me riding lessons if I would help them learn the song."

Surprise flickered in his eyes. "That's the reason you've been coming out to ride?"

"The opportunity was too good to pass up. I wanted to ride again for a long time. They wanted to learn the song. This seemed the perfect arrangement."

It *had* been perfect, until she made the mistake of falling hard for the boys—and for their father.

"Well, thank you. Every time I hear that song now, I'll remember them...and you."

Before she could answer, Rafe Santiago came over looking harried. "It's crazy out there. Several people have decided to leave their vehicles here and come back for them when the storm passes, so we've got even more to take home. Do you think you could take home Martha Valentine and Ann and Max Watts? They all live on the same street near the park."

"Absolutely." He turned to her. "Are you sure you don't mind taking the boys home? That would help."

"No problem. I'll get them home safely," she promised.

"Thanks."

He gave her one more smile then turned to take care of his responsibilities.

That was just the kind of guy he was. When something needed doing, he would just tip his hat back and go to work.

It was one of the many reasons she loved him.

She couldn't stand here mooning over him when she had her own responsibilities, people who needed her. After one last look at him helping the frail Martha Valentine into her coat with a gentleness that brought tears to her eyes, she turned away to gather up her own charges.

The storm was worse than she had imagined.

The moment they stepped out of the St. Nicholas Lodge, snow blew at them from every direction and the wind nearly toppled them over. Everyone was huddling inside their winter coats as they made their way through the deepening drifts to the parking lot.

"Boys, grab hold of me and my father so you don't blow away." She had to raise her voice to be heard over the whining wind. She wasn't really worried about that, but needed their help more to support her father—something she couldn't tell him.

Fortunately, her vehicle was parked close to the entry and it only took them a few moments.

She opened the driver's side first so she could start the engine to warm up the heater and defrost, then hurried around to help her father inside. Her SUV passenger seat was just a little too high for him and Curt didn't have enough strength to pull himself into it alone.

"Thanks," he muttered when she gave him a boost, clearly embarrassed about needing help.

By the time he was settled and the twins were buckled into the back seat, Ella was frozen through from that icy wind—and she still had to brush the snow from the windows so she could see to drive.

Finally, they were on their way. She took off at a ponderous pace, her shoulders taut and her hands gripping the steering wheel. She could hardly see through the blinding snow that blew across the windshield much faster than her wipers could handle.

Her father looked out the window at the relentless snow while the boys, oblivious to the storm outside or the tension inside, chattered to each other about the show and the approaching holidays.

"We had about ten people tell us our song was the best one," Trevor said proudly.

"You did a great job," she said, tightening her fingers on the wheel as a particularly strong gust of wind shook the vehicle and sent snow flying into the windshield.

Usually she didn't mind driving in a storm, but this was coming down so fast. Coupled with the wind and blowing snow, it made visibility basically zero.

"Can we listen to the radio?" Colter asked.

"I need to concentrate right now. Can you just hum to yourselves?"

"We can sing our song again," the boys offered.

"I'd like that," Curt said, to her surprise.

While her eyes were glued to the road, she was vaguely aware from her peripheral vision that he had half turned in his seat to face the twins. "I always loved that song. You boys *were* the best thing on the show," he told them.

She couldn't spare a look in the rearview mirror right now. If she did, she was sure the twins would be grinning.

"We'll have to do it without the guitar," Trevor warned.

"That's okay. You can sing without it." Her father turned to her and spoke with a guarded tone. "That won't be too stressful for you while you're driving, will it?"

She shook her head and the boys started singing the song she had heard them practice so many times before. There was something special about this time, in the warm shelter of her vehicle while the storm raged outside.

"That was wonderful," her father said when they finished, his voice gruff. "I'm sure your dad loved it."

"He did," Trevor said. "He came and found us after and gave us big hugs and said he was so proud of us and had never been so touched."

"He said it was the best gift anybody ever gave him," Colter added. "He said it made him cry and that there's nothing wrong with a guy crying when something makes him too happy to hold it in! Can you believe that?"

She didn't answer as she felt emotion bubble up in her chest.

"It's a good song," her father said gruffly.

"Want us to sing another one? We can do 'Jingle Bells' or 'Rudolph' or 'Away in a Manger.'"

"Sure. We'll have our own private Christmas show," Curt said.

The boys launched into song and she was grateful to her father for distracting them so she could focus on driving.

She could usually make it between The Christmas Ranch and the Broken Arrow in about ten minutes, but she was creeping along at a snail's pace because of the weather conditions.

"Almost there," she finally said after about a half hour. "Your turnoff should be just ahead."

At least she was fairly certain. It was hard to be sure with the poor visibility and the heavy snow making everything look alien and *wrong* somehow.

She turned her signal on, though she couldn't see any lights in either direction, when suddenly her own headlights caught something big and dark on the middle of the road just ahead of them.

It was an animal of some kind. A cow or horse or moose. She couldn't be sure and it really wouldn't matter when two thousand pounds of animal came through the windshield.

Reflexively, she slammed the brakes. She wasn't going fast at all but the road was slick, coated in a thick layer of ice, and the tires couldn't seem to catch. The vehicle fishtailed dangerously and she fought to regain control.

She tried to turn the wheel frantically, with no success. It was a terrible feeling, to be behind the wheel of a vehicle she had absolutely no control over.

"Hang on," she called.

The boys screamed and her father swore as the vehicle

went down a small embankment and into a snowbank about ten feet down.

Her heartbeat raced like she had just finished an Olympic sprint and her stomach twirled in an awful imitation of her wheels spinning out of control.

"Is everybody okay?" she asked.

"Yeah," her dad said gruffly. "Gave me a hell of a start."

"We're okay," Trevor said.

She turned around to reassure herself but all she could see in the darkness were their wide eyes.

"Are we stuck?" Colter asked.

She tightened her shaking fingers on the steering wheel. "I don't know. I haven't tried to get us out yet. You're sure you're both all right?"

"Yeah. It was like the Tilt-A-Whirl at the county fair."

Now she remembered why she had always hated that ride.

"Well, that was fun. Let's get everybody home."

Ella put the vehicle in Reverse and accelerated but the wheels just spun. The snow was too deep here for them to find purchase. She pulled forward a little, then tried to reverse again. She thought she made a little progress but, again, the SUV couldn't pass a certain point.

She went through the same process several times until her father finally stopped her. "You're only making things worse," he said. "Face it. With that incline, this thing doesn't have the horsepower, at least not in Reverse. We're going to need somebody to pull us out."

The boys had fallen silent in the back and she could tell they were beginning to grasp the seriousness of the situation.

It could be hours before someone came by. As the snow piled up, their tracks would quickly be wiped away.

She could still call for help. She could tell Beck how to find them. She reached for her purse and fumbled for her cell phone, scrolling through until she found his number.

She tried to connect but the call didn't go through that time, or the second time she tried.

"What's wrong?" her father asked.

"Why don't I have any service?" she wailed.

"Must be in one of the dead zones around here."

Naturally. It was just her luck to get stuck in one of the few places where she couldn't call for help. "What about yours, Dad?"

"I didn't bring it."

"Why on earth not?"

He didn't answer for a long moment, then shrugged. "What's the point? You know I can't work that damn thing very well."

He could barely hold it in his trembling hands. Hitting the numbers was even harder. She had tried to coach him through speech-to-text methods but he couldn't quite master it.

It wouldn't make much difference. They had the same carrier. If she didn't have service, he likely wouldn't, either.

That gave her very few options.

"In that case, I don't see a choice," she said after a moment of considering them. "I better head to the Broken Arrow for help. Jax and Dan are there. Somebody should be able to pull us out with the one of the ranch tractors."

"You can't wander around in that storm. Just wait here. Beck will be home soon."

"Yes, but all the people he was taking home live south

of here, which means he'll likely be coming to the ranch from the other direction. He won't even pass this way."

"When he sees the boys haven't made it home, don't you think he'll come looking for us?"

"Probably." That did make sense and provided some comfort to the worry and grave sense of responsibility she was feeling for the others in her vehicle. "The problem is, he might be shuttling multiple groups of people home. I have no idea how long he'll be at it, and to be honest, I don't feel good about waiting here, Dad. The snow keeps piling up and the temperature is dropping. I need to get you and the twins home where it's safe. The fastest way to do that is to walk to the ranch house. It can't be far. I can be there and back with help in no time."

"I don't like it."

What else was new? She could write a book about the things her father didn't like about her, apparently.

"I'm sorry, but right now I have bigger things to worry about than your opinion of me," she said, more sharply than she intended.

Curt opened his mouth, then closed it again. Good. She didn't have time to argue with him.

"I need you to stay here with the boys and watch over them. I have a full tank of gas. I'll make sure there's no snow obstructing the exhaust, so no worries about carbon monoxide building up inside. You should be fine to keep the engine running and the heater on."

"We can come with you," Colter said.

She had no doubt that the boys would be able to keep up with her. Her father, on the other hand, would not, and she didn't want to leave him here alone.

Torn, she gazed at all three of them. She didn't want to go out into that storm but she didn't dare take her chances of Beck miraculously just stumbling onto them. From the road above, they would be impossible to spot once the snow obscured their tracks, especially with that blowing wind and poor visibility.

This was serious, she realized. This country could be unforgiving and harsh and she would have to draw on all her reserves of strength to help them get through this.

"I need you boys to stay here where it's warm. Do what my dad says, okay? I'll be back shortly."

"Here. Take my coat. It's heavier than yours," Curt said gruffly.

"Mine is plenty warm. You might need yours. I will take the flashlight in the glove box, though."

She reached across him to get it out, grateful she had changed the batteries to fresh ones a few weeks earlier.

"In the back, there's a bag filled with bottled water, some granola bars and a couple of emergency blankets. You're probably not going to need them, but you should know about them, just in case."

"You're prepared," her father said, surprise in his voice.

"I have a father who taught me well about the harshness of Idaho winters."

She wanted to tell him she could learn all sorts of things, if only he were willing to teach her, but this wasn't the time to rehash that argument.

"Sounds like a smart man," he said after a moment.

"About some things, anyway," she said tartly.

Focused on the job at hand, she wrapped her scarf around her face and buttoned up her coat. "I'm going to give you my phone. You don't have cell service here but if I'm not back in a timely manner, you can try climbing up the incline and see if you have better service up there. Give me half an hour to get help first, though. I would rather you didn't leave the vehicle."

After a tense moment, her father finally nodded. "Be careful. I've only got the one daughter, and I'm fairly fond of her."

His words made tears thicken in her throat. Why did he have to be so stubborn?

"I'll be careful. You, too. See you in a little bit." She paused. "I love you, Dad."

She climbed out of the vehicle and whatever he said in response was snatched away by the howling wind that bit through her clothing and stung her face like a thousand knives.

She slipped several times as she tried to make it up the slight hill. Her boots were lined and warm but they weren't meant for heavy-duty hiking, more for walking through the snowy streets of Boston.

By the time she made it back to the road, she was already out of breath and perspiring inside her coat. She stood for a moment to catch her bearings. Everything was disorienting. White upon white upon white.

Fear was heavy on her shoulders. This was serious, she thought again. She had heard horror stories of people being lost in blizzards, their frozen corpses only found months later. Perhaps she would have been better off staying in the car.

But even now, knowing it was just below her, she could hardly see her SUV. Someone with no idea what had happened to them would never find it.

She headed off in the direction of the ranch house, tucking her chin in against the wind, praying she didn't miss his driveway and struggling step by step through the deepening snow.

It was much harder going than she had imagined, but she remained solely focused on doing what she had to, to save her father and the twins.

Shouldn't she have found the ranch road by now?

Panic began to flutter through her. She had to be close, but where was it? She couldn't even see the roadway anymore. She was almost certain she was still on it, but what if she wasn't? What if she had somehow taken a wrong turn and was somehow heading in the wrong direction? She would die out here—and her father and the twins would eventually run out of gas and would freeze to death, too.

What had she done? She should never have trusted her instincts. She should have stayed in the SUV with Curt and the twins. Had she doomed them all?

The panic ratcheted up and she tried frantically to see if she could find a light, a landmark, anything. All she could see was white.

Dear God, she prayed. *Please help me.*

The only answer was the constant whine of the wind churning the snow around her.

She had to keep moving. This had to be the way. There. Was that a light? She peered through the darkness to a spot set back from the road about the correct distance to be the Broken Arrow ranch house.

Was that the log arch over his driveway? She thought so but couldn't quite be sure. Instinct had her moving in that direction, when suddenly a dark shape again loomed out of the darkness.

Ella's instinctive scream tangled in her throat as the dark shape trotted closer. In her flashlight's glow, she suddenly recognized the calm, familiar features of an old friend.

She had never been so very grateful to see another living soul.

"Creampuff! What are you doing out here?" Ella exclaimed. At her voice, the horse ambled closer.

She must have somehow gotten out. She remembered the boys telling her the horse could be an escape artist. Why on earth would she have chosen this particular moment to get out?

Was Creampuff the thing she had almost hit on the road, the shape that had frightened her into hitting the brakes and sliding off the road?

Ella didn't like the consequences, but she was very grateful she hadn't hit the horse.

"You shouldn't be out here," she said to the horse. "It's dangerous."

Creampuff whickered and nudged at her. She seemed happy to see Ella, too.

She suddenly had an idea. It was completely impractical, but if it worked, it might be the answer to her current dilemma.

The storm was so disorienting, she was worried that she would end up miles from her destination. What were the chances that the horse could get her to Beckett's ranch house?

It was worth a try. Better than wandering aimlessly out here on her own. The only trick would be mounting up without a saddle, stirrups or reins—especially when she could barely manage it when she had all those necessary items.

The horse would lead her back to the barn on the Broken Arrow. Somehow she knew it.

If she wanted to save her father and the twins, she had to try.

Chapter Thirteen

"What the hell do you mean, they're not here? They left forty-five minutes before I did!"

Beckett stared at his brother, fear settling like jagged shards of ice in his gut.

"I don't know what to tell you. Nobody is here but Dan and me. We haven't seen a soul. Maybe she took them to her ranch house instead."

Wouldn't she have called him if her plans had changed? He couldn't believe she would simply abscond with his children with no word.

Those ice shards twisted. "Something's wrong."

"You don't know that," Jax said, his tone placating.

"I do. Something's wrong. They should have been here half an hour ago. They're in trouble."

Jax started to look concerned. "Before you run off, why don't you try to call them?"

Good idea. "You call the Baker's Dozen. I'll try their cell phones."

He dialed Curt's first and it went immediately to voice mail. He left a short message, telling the man to call him when he heard the message, then tried Ella's. It rang twice and he thought it would be connected but it shortly went to voice mail, too.

"No answer at the ranch," Jax said. He was beginning to look concerned, as well.

Beck had just spent an hour driving through these terrible conditions. He knew how bad it was out there—just as he knew Ella and her father had left with the boys well before he could load his first group of senior citizens into his vehicle to take them home.

Something was wrong. He knew it in his bones.

He hung up the phone after leaving her a terse message, as well, then faced his brother.

"I'm going to look for them. Call me if they show up."

Jax was smart enough to know when to not argue. He nodded. "What do you need me to do?"

"Stay in touch. For now, that's all."

He rushed out the door, doing his best to ignore the panic. He knew what could happen under these conditions. A few years ago, a rancher up north of them had gotten lost in a blizzard like this and ended up freezing to death just a few feet from his own back door.

The storm hadn't abated a whit in the few minutes he'd been inside. It whistled down through the mountains like a wild banshee. This was going to be one hell of a white Christmas. No doubt about it. He wouldn't be surprised if they ended up with at least two or three feet out of one storm, with much deeper drifts in spots from that wind.

He headed down the long, winding driveway, his heart in his throat and a prayer on his lips.

He had just started down the driveway when his headlights flashed on something dark and massive heading straight for him. If he had been going any faster, he would have inevitably hit it. As it was, he had to tap his brakes, even in four-wheel-drive low, to come to a stop.

It was a horse, he realized as he muscled the truck to a stop and his eyes adjusted to the shifting light conditions.

A horse carrying a rider!

What in the world? Who would be crazy enough to go riding on a night like tonight?

He yanked open his door and stepped out of his truck, boots crunching in calf-high snow, even though Jax had already cleared the driveway once that night.

"Beck! Oh, Beck. I'm so happy to see you!"

"Ella!" he exclaimed.

She jumped off of the horse and slipped to the ground and an instant later, she was in his arms. He didn't know if he had surged forward or if she had rushed to him, but he held her tightly as she trembled violently in the cold.

"What's happened?" he demanded. "Where are the boys?"

Her voice trembled. "I—I slid into a ditch back on the r-road. I don't know how far b-back. I thought it was closer b-but it seemed like f-forever that I w-walked."

"Why were you walking in the first place? Why didn't you call me to come find you?"

"I t-tried. I didn't have cell service. We're off the road, out of sight. E-even if someone t-tried to find us, they wouldn't be able to. I—I knew I had to f-find help, but I think I must have been lost or missed the road or something. I was panicking but I—I prayed and suddenly Creampuff appeared."

She shivered out a sob that made his arms tighten around her. For just a moment, she rested her cheek against him and he wanted to stay keep her safe and warm in his arms forever.

"It f-felt like some kind of m-miracle."

She was a miracle. She was amazing. If she hadn't faced her fear of horses, she might be wandering out there still. Somehow she had found the strength to climb on a horse without tack or saddle and made her way here, to him.

What would he have done if Creampuff hadn't found her, if she was still wandering around out there, lost in the storm?

He couldn't bear to think about it. If anything had happened to her, it would shatter him. His arms tightened as the feelings he had been fighting for weeks burst to the surface.

He shoved them back down, knowing this wasn't the time or the place to deal with them.

"You're frozen. Let's get you up to the house."

"No! I—I have to show you where to find my dad and the boys. You'll never see my car from the road."

She was so certain of that, he had to accept she was right. "At least hop inside the truck while I put Creampuff in the barn. Jax can take care of her. She deserves extra oats after tonight."

He helped her inside his cab—something he should have done the moment she hopped off that horse, he realized with self-disgust. The heater was blasting and he found the emergency blanket behind the seat and tucked it around her.

"We have to hurry."

"We will. This will only take a moment, I promise."

He closed the door and called his brother as he led the heroic Creampuff toward the barn, thirty yards away.

"Need my help?"

"Maybe. Not yet. Take care of Creampuff for me and give her all the crab apples she wants right now. I'll stay in touch."

He hurried back out to his truck through the storm, trying not to think about how very close they had come to a tragedy he couldn't bear to think about.

Ella had never been so cold, despite the blanket and the blessed warmth pouring full-blast from the heater of Beck's pickup. Occasional shivers still racked her body and Beck continued casting worried looks her way.

"How much farther?" he asked.

She peered out the window at the landscape that seemed familiar but not familiar. Everything was white, blurred by blowing snow.

She recognized that fence line there, and the curve ahead, and knew they had to be close but she could see no sign of her SUV.

"There!" she suddenly exclaimed. "Down there, just ahead. See the glow of my taillights?"

He tapped his brakes and brought the truck to a stop. "Wow. You were right. There are no tracks left on the road and it's well out of view from up here. If you hadn't pointed it out, I would have missed it."

"The engine is still running. I had a full tank of gas so they should have had enough for a few more hours."

He opened his door and frowned when she opened

hers, too. "Ella, stay here. You're still half-frozen. I'll get them."

She shook her head. "Dad's going to need help getting up that little slope. It might take both of us."

Her father had grown so frail this past year that she suspected Beck could carry the other man up the slope over his shoulder in a fireman's carry without even having to catch his breath, but after a moment he nodded.

"I'm sorry you'll have to go out in the cold again."

"Only temporarily. I'll be okay."

She opened her door before he could argue further and climbed out, then headed down the slight slope to her snow-covered SUV.

The door opened before she could reach it and her father stuck his head out.

"Ella? Is that you?" he called, peering into the snowy darkness.

"Yes."

"Oh, thank heavens. I've been worried sick," he exclaimed.

With good reason, she acknowledged. She could have died out there—and there was a very good chance her father and the boys might have, too, before help could arrive.

"I brought Beck."

"I knew you could do it."

"How are the boys?" she asked as she reached the vehicle, with Beck right behind her.

"See for yourself," her father said. "They're sound asleep."

Sure enough, the boys were cuddled together under one of her emergency blankets.

Colter was the first one to open his eyes. He blinked

at her sleepily, then his gaze caught his father, just behind her.

"Hey, Dad!" Colter smiled. "I think I fell asleep."

"Looks like it. We'll get you to the truck and then
home in no time."

"Okay." He yawned, then shook his brother awake.
Trevor looked just as happy to see both of them. Neither
boy seemed the worse for wear after their ordeal.

"Boys, let's get you back to the truck. It's probably
better if I carry you, since your cowboy boots aren't the
best for snow. Ella, why don't you stay here where it's
warm for a few moments?"

She wanted to offer to take one of the boys and then
come back down to help her father, but she wasn't sure
she would have the strength to make that trip twice more.

"Me first," Trevor said.

Beck scooped him up onto his back and Ella slid into
his warm spot as they headed up the slope. In seconds,
the still-blowing snow obscured their shapes from view.

"You guys did okay?" she asked Colter.

He nodded. "You were gone a long time."

"I know. I'm sorry. I had some complications."

"We sang just about every song we knew, then Mr.
Baker told us stories about Christmas when he was a kid."

He started reciting a few of the stories, one she remembered her father telling her and another that seemed
new. Maybe Curt had told it to her once, but it had been
lost along with everything else the summer she was eight.

It seemed like forever but had probably been only two
or three minutes when Beck opened the door. "Okay,
kid. You're next."

He repeated the process with Colter, leaving her alone
with her father.

"You sure you're okay?" Curt said, his voice gruff.

"I got lost. You were right. I probably should have stayed with you until the help arrived."

"That's funny. I was about to say *you* were right. Nobody would have found us until morning, when it would have been too late."

She was spared from having to imagine all the grim possibilities when Beck opened the door.

"Turn off your engine and bring along the key."

"What about my SUV?"

"Jax and I can come down and pull it out after I get you home."

She nodded and did as he said, hoping he would be able to find it again without the gleam of the taillights to light the way.

"I wish I could give you a piggyback ride, too," Beck said to her father.

"I'll be fine. I just need a little support."

In the end, Beck all but carried her father, anyway. She was deeply grateful for his solid strength but also for the gentle way he tried to spare her father's pride as he helped him into the truck's passenger seat. Once he was settled, Ella slipped into the back seat of the crew cab pickup with the boys and Beck headed for the Baker's Dozen, driving with slow care.

Just before he reached their turnoff, she heard her phone's ringtone distantly. It took her a moment to remember it was in her father's pocket. He fumbled with it but finally managed to pull it out. Before he could hand it over, Curt checked out the display with the caller ID.

"It's Manny. Wonder why he's calling you?"

"Maybe because you usually leave your cell phone at home," she replied, reaching over the seat for her phone.

"Do you know where your padre is?" the foreman asked as soon as she answered. "Is he with you?"

"Yes. We've had a rough evening but should be home soon. Beck is bringing us."

"He can't. Turn around."

"Turn around? Why?"

"You can't get through. One of the big pines along the driveway blew over in the wind and there's no way around it. It's a good thing nobody was driving under it when it fell."

"What's going on?" Beck asked, coming to a slow stop just before the turn.

"The driveway is blocked. We won't be able to get through."

Could this evening get any worse? First she ran off the road, now they were stranded away from home.

"Okay. No problem," Beck answered. "You can just come back to the Broken Arrow with us. I'll feel better about that, anyway."

"Will you be okay for tonight?" Manny asked.

"I suppose," she answered, though she dreaded the prospect. "What about you?" she asked the foreman. "You're stuck on the ranch."

"We're fine. We have plenty of food and so far the electricity is still on. I can take care of everything up here, as long as I know the two of you are safe and have a place to sleep."

"Thanks, Manny. Be safe."

"Same to you."

She hung up. "I guess we're spending the night at the Broken Arrow, if that's okay with you."

"Just fine."

He turned the pickup around slowly and began inching back to his own ranch.

"Dad, what about your prescriptions?" Ella asked, as the thought suddenly occurred to her.

"I took my evening pills before I went to the show, since I wasn't sure what time we'd be back. I'll be fine."

"You're staying at our house?" Trevor asked, excitement in his voice.

"You can have our beds," Colter offered. "Only someone will have to sleep on the top bunk."

"We have plenty of space," Beckett assured them. "We don't have to kick anybody out of bed. We've got a couple spare bedrooms and a comfortable sofa in the family room. You're more than welcome, and in the morning we can head over with chainsaws and clear a path."

"Thank you," she murmured. She really didn't want to spend the night at his house, but unless she wanted to take another merciless trudge through that storm, she didn't see that they had any choice.

"Are you sure you're okay, Dad? Is there anything else I can get you?"

An hour later, she stood in a comfortable guest room with a leather recliner, a wide bed and a flat-screen TV. Her father was already stretched out on the bed with a remote and a glass of water. He wore his own shirt and a pair of pajama bottoms borrowed from Beck's uncle.

She wore another pair, but they were about six sizes too big, baggy and long.

"I don't think so. I haven't been this tired in a long time. I'm probably going to crash the minute the news is over."

If not before. Curt had become good at dozing off while the television still played.

"All right. Good night." She leaned in to kiss his stubbly cheek. As she turned to go, she was surprised when Curt reached his trembling fingers out to touch her arm.

"I didn't say this earlier, but...I was proud of you tonight."

Her father's unexpected words sent a soft warmth seeping through her. "Thank you. I'm happy you enjoyed the program, but it was the children who did all the work."

"I'm not talking about the show, though that was excellent, too. I meant later. When you went to find help. You risked your life for me and those twins of Beckett's. I was never more proud to call you my daughter."

He gave her arm a squeeze and she looked down, wanting to wrap his liver-spotted, trembling fingers in hers and tuck them against her cheek.

"I can do all sorts of things, if you only give me the chance," she said softly.

His hand stiffened and he pulled it away. "You're talking about running the ranch again."

Stupid. She wanted to kick herself. Why bring up a point of contention and ruin what had been a rare, lovely, peaceful moment between them?

"Yes. I am talking about running the ranch. I want to. Why won't you even give me the chance?"

To her chagrin, her voice wobbled on the last word. Exhaustion, she told herself. Still, she couldn't seem to hold back the torrent of emotions. "No matter what I do, you can't see me as anything but the silly girl who fell off a horse."

"You were in a coma for weeks. You nearly died."

"But I didn't! I survived."

"More than that," he said gruffly. "You thrived, especially after your mother took you away from here."

She stared, speechless at his words. "Is that what you think?" she asked, when she could trust her voice. "That I only thrived because Mom took me back to Boston? I grieved every day I was away. I love it here, Dad. I came back, didn't I?"

"To care for a feeble old man. Not because you belong here."

"The ranch is part of me, no matter what you say."

"So is Boston! You have a life there. I can't ask you to give up everything that's important to you. You love music—the opera, the symphony. Not J. D. Wyatt and his Warbling Wranglers. You belong to a different world."

"Yes, I love those things you mentioned. But I also love J.D. and George Jones and Emmylou Harris. The music you and I listened to together. Why can't I have both? Why do I have to choose?"

He appeared struck by this, his brow furrowed as he considered her words. She didn't know what might be different this time, when they had had similar arguments before, but something she said seemed to be trickling through his stubbornness.

"Honey, you don't know anything about running the ranch." She might have been imagining it, but his voice sounded a little less certain.

"You can teach me, Dad. I've been telling you that for months. There's no better time than now. I want to learn from you, while you're still here to teach me. This is my heritage, half of what makes me who I am. I don't understand why you can't see that."

He appeared struck by her words and she decided to

quit while she was ahead. Perhaps she had given him something to think about—but why should this time make the difference when all those other times hadn't?

"I don't want to fight with you, Dad. It's been a long day. Can we agree to focus on the holidays and talk about this again after Christmas?"

"That sounds like a good idea." Her father paused. "I love you, you know. No matter what else you think. I love you and I've always been proud of you."

Tears welled up in her throat at this hard, stubborn man she had considered her hero all of her life. "I love you, too, Dad. Get some rest."

Beck slipped into his own room across the hall as he heard her last words and realized she would be coming out at any moment. He didn't want her to leave her father's guest room and find him standing outside the door.

He hadn't meant to eavesdrop, had only been there to check on his guests and see if they needed anything. The slightly raised voices had drawn his attention and he stopped, not wanting to walk in on an argument between Ella and her father.

This is my heritage, half of what makes me who I am. I don't understand why you can't see that.

Her words seemed to howl through his mind like that wind, resonating with truth.

He couldn't buy the ranch out from under her.

Beck leaned against his bedpost as the assurance settled deep in his chest. On paper, purchasing the Baker's Dozen was the smart play. He needed to expand his own operations and grow the Broken Arrow and it made perfect sense to merge the two ranches.

A month ago, he would have jumped at the chance

without a second thought, assuming Ella had no interest in ranching and would be happy to take the money and run back to Boston.

He knew better now. He knew her hopes and her dreams and her yearnings. He had seen her face when they went on that ride into the backcountry as she looked at her family's land from the foothills. He had watched her tackle her own fear of horses in order to prove her own mettle. He had seen the courage she showed during a blizzard, her willingness to put her own comfort and safety at risk to help those she loved.

Her heart would break if Curt sold the ranch out from under her.

Beck couldn't do that to her.

He loved her too much.

The truth seemed to blow through him with all the impact of that storm rattling the windows of his room, crashing over him as if he were standing directly under the big pine that had fallen on the Baker's Dozen.

He loved Ella Baker.

He loved her sweetness, her grace, the gentle care she took with his sons. He loved her sense of humor and her grit and the soft, sexy noises she made when he kissed her.

He loved her.

What in heaven's name was he supposed to do about that now?

He assumed the normal course of action in this sort of situation would be to tell the woman in question about his feelings and see if she might share them—or at least see if she didn't reject them outright.

This wasn't a typical situation.

He thought of the precious gift she had helped his

boys give him that day, the song that always touched him about a cowboy being alone on Christmas. He didn't want to be alone, like that cowboy. He wanted sweetness and warmth and a woman's smile, just for him.

He wanted Ella.

Did he have the courage to try again? His marriage had left him uncertain about his own instincts, completely aware of all the ways he had screwed up.

He couldn't afford to make a disastrous mistake like that again, but something told him with sweet certainty that allowing himself to love Ella could never be anything but perfect.

She filled his life with joy and wonder, reminded him of everything good and right in his world.

His boys loved her, too. They had thrived under her loving care, in a way he hadn't seen them do with anyone else. Somehow, she had managed to reach them, to sand away a few of their rough edges.

They needed that in their lives. *He* did, too.

Could he find the strength and courage to overlook all the ugliness of his past to build a brighter future with Ella?

As he stood in his bedroom with the storm raging outside, he wasn't sure he knew the answer to that.

He still hadn't figured it out an hour later as he finally settled the boys for the night and closed the door to their room, confident they were finally asleep.

The combined excitement of their stellar performance at the Christmas show, being trapped in a snowbank during the blizzard and then having their favorite teacher staying in their house seemed to have made sleep elusive, but exhaustion at last had claimed them.

It was late, past midnight, but they could sleep in the next day. He had already received an alert that school would be canceled tomorrow because of the storm, still raging throughout the region. It hadn't surprised him. Nobody would be able to get through on the roads out there until at least noon or later.

He needed to sleep, too. The next day was bound to be a busy one and would start early.

Like his sons, though, he felt too wired to sleep. He had a feeling that if he tried to climb into bed now, he would only toss and turn.

His thoughts were in tumult and he still didn't know what to do about Ella and his feelings for her. Meantime, he decided to grab a drink of water and maybe one of those cookies a neighbor brought over earlier, then head into his ranch office to catch up on paperwork.

He was heading through the great room toward the kitchen when he spotted someone sitting in the darkness, just out of reach of the glow emanating from the Christmas tree and the dying embers of the fire burning in the hearth.

His gaze sharpened when he realized it was Ella. He had almost missed her.

Had she fallen asleep out here? Her day had been more strenuous than anyone's, between orchestrating that amazing performance earlier, then rescuing her father and the boys.

What was she doing out here? Was she all right?"

Her face was in shadows but he thought he glimpsed the streak of tears on her cheeks, reflecting the colored Christmas lights. As he moved closer, she must have sensed his presence. She looked up then quickly away but not before he was able to confirm his suspicion.

She was crying.

"Oh. You startled me." She swiped her cheeks and kept her face averted, obviously trying to hide them from him. He was torn between wanting to respect her obvious desire for privacy and being unable to bear the thought of her hurting.

Finally he sat beside her on the sofa. "El. What is it? What's wrong?"

"Nothing. I'm fine. It's just…been a long day."

"You need to be in bed. Why are you sitting out here by yourself?" *Crying*, he added silently.

She sighed. "Do you ever have those times when it feels like your mind is spinning so fast you can't keep up with it?"

"All the time. If it's not the ranch I'm worrying about, it's the boys or Jax or Uncle Dan."

Or her father, he wanted to add, but didn't want to upset her more. Most likely, that conversation with Curt was the reason for these tears.

He couldn't bear them, especially when he had the ability to dry them right here, right now.

"Ella, I don't—"

"Beck, I have to—"

They started to speak at the same time, then both faltered. After an awkward little moment, she gestured to him. "It's your house. You first."

He wanted to argue, but couldn't see any point. Better to tell her what was on his mind as quickly as he could.

"You should know, I've decided to tell your father I won't be purchasing the Baker's Dozen."

Her eyes looked huge in the multicolored light from the tree as she stared at him. "You *what*?"

"It was early days in the discussions between us.

Whatever you heard today when he and I were talking, nothing has been signed. There's no breach of contract or anything. So I'm officially backing out. I won't buy it."

"But...I don't understand. I thought you needed the watering rights and the pasture land to expand your operations."

"I do. I will, someday, but I'll figure something out when the need is more critical."

"Why?"

He needed to expand the Broken Arrow, but he couldn't do it in good conscience by buying her father's land out from under her.

"You should be running your family's ranch, Ella."

She made a disbelieving sound and though he feared it might be a mistake, he reached for her hand. "You are perfectly capable. You've got exactly all the traits it takes to make a go of things out here. You're tough, spunky and bold. You're willing to learn and you're not afraid to ask for help when you need it. You've shown all those things, again and again. Your father knows it, too—it's just taking him longer than it should to admit it."

Her fingers trembled in his as if she were still cold, and he wanted to wrap her in his arms until her shivering ceased.

"I don't understand," she finally said.

"What's to understand? I'm withdrawing my tentative agreement to purchase the property. It's yours. Curt can show you how to run it, just like he helped me figure things out here after my father died. If he doesn't, *I* will show you the ropes and find other local ranchers to do the same. Wade Dalton. Chase and Faith Brannon. Justin Hartford. You have good neighbors who will want nothing more than to see you succeed."

In the light of the Christmas tree, he saw something bright and joyful flash across her expression—hope and an eagerness to prove herself. For one beautiful instant, she looked exactly what she was, strong and capable of anything.

That's why he was doubly shocked after a moment when she pulled her hand away from his and rose as if to put space between them.

"I don't think I can do that."

"Why not? There's not a single doubt in my mind you'll make a go of it, with or without your father's help."

She gave him one quick look, her lips pressed together and her chin quivering, then she shook her head.

"I…can't. I'm not staying here. I've made up my mind to return to Boston right after Christmas."

Shock tangled his thoughts and his words. Had he misheard her? Not an hour ago, she had pleaded with her father to give her a chance at running the Baker's Dozen and now she was turning tail and taking off? What in Hades had happened?

"Why would you do that? I just told you that I won't be making an offer on the ranch—and I'll make sure nobody else around here does, either. There won't be much I can do about things if Curt decides to sell to an outsider, but I don't think that's what your dad wants, anyway."

As he watched, another tear dripped down her cheek, iridescent in the Christmas tree lights.

"I can't do it," she whispered.

"Are you kidding me? You can do any damn thing you put your mind to. You tamed the twin terrors, didn't you?"

He meant his words as a joke. It seemed to fall flat and she hitched in a breath that sounded more like a sob.

"That's why I...can't stay. Because of the boys and—and you."

Another tear dripped. He couldn't bear this. What had he done to offend her so grievously that she couldn't even stand to stay in the same county with him? He would fix it, whatever it was.

He rose. "I'm sorry. You're going to have to forgive me for being a big, dumb cowboy, but I don't know what the heck you're talking about."

She didn't answer him for several moments, the only sound the relentless wind and the click of branches from the red-twigged dogwoods outside the window.

Finally she swallowed. "I have come to...care deeply for—for Trevor and Colter. I don't see how I could continue to live here, always stuck on the edges of your, er, *their* lives. Just the nice neighbor who once taught them how to sing a song for their dad. I don't want that. I—I want more."

He couldn't catch his breath, suddenly. She was talking about the boys, right? Or did she mean something else? "Ella."

She didn't meet his gaze. "I'm sorry. Forget I said anything. I shouldn't have. It's late and I'm tired and not thinking straight. I'll go to bed now."

She tried to slip past him but he couldn't let her. Not yet. He blocked her path, never more grateful for his size than he was in that moment. "Stop. What are you saying?"

"It doesn't matter."

He tipped up her chin, until she had no choice but to look at him, his strong, amazing Ella. "I think it matters more than anything else in my world right now."

Her mouth wobbled a little again, then tightened with belligerence. "Do you want me to completely humiliate myself? Why not? I've already made a complete fool of myself. Fine. I'll say it. I'm in love with you. Are you happy now?"

She hadn't finished the words before he kissed her fiercely, pouring out all the emotions he had been fighting for weeks. Months, he realized. He had fallen for her when she first came back to Pine Gulch to stay with her father, he just hadn't been able to admit it to himself until now.

He kissed her until they were both breathing hard and the room was beginning to spin and he wasn't sure he would ever be able to bring himself to move from this spot.

"Does that answer your question?" he finally asked against her mouth. Joy continued to pulse through him, bright and shining and as beautiful as any Christmas tree. "*Happy* doesn't begin to cover how I feel to know the woman I love with all my heart shares a little of my feelings."

She stared at him, shock warring with the arousal in her eyes. "You love me? That's impossible."

"Need another demonstration?" He kissed her again, this time with a sweet, aching tenderness he felt from the depths of his soul. He lowered them to the sofa and held her on his lap, teasing and touching and tasting.

"I guess that wasn't really an answer, was it?" he murmured, after another long moment. "Kisses are wonderful, don't get me wrong, but any guy who's attracted to you—which would have to be every sane guy with a pulse—could give you those."

She swallowed, her hands tangled in his hair and her lips swollen from his mouth. "That's right." Her voice sounded thready, low, and made him ache all over again.

"You'll have to be more persuasive than that if you expect me to believe you want me and not my father's ranch."

He tightened his arms around her, loving this playful side of her. As he gazed at her eyes reflecting the lights of the Christmas tree, he thought that he had never loved the holidays so very much as he did right now, with his own Christmas miracle in his arms.

"I stand by what I said before. I don't want the Baker's Dozen, and I'll be sure to tell Curt that as soon as I get the chance. We can go wake him up, if you want."

"You really think I would be stupid enough to want to wake my father up right now? I'm a little busy here," she said, pressing her mouth to his jawline in a way that made his breath catch and everything inside him want to slide over her to show her just what her teasing did to him.

He gazed into her eyes, hoping she could see he meant his words. "Curt will come to his senses. I'll make sure of it. As far as I'm concerned, that ranch is yours, to do with as you see fit. If you want to sell all the cattle and start raising alpacas, that's your business."

Beck decided he wouldn't mind spending the rest of his life trying to make that soft, sweet smile appear again.

"I do love alpacas," she murmured. "They're so much cuter than cattle—and think of all the adorable Christmas sweaters I could make out of their wool."

"I can picture it now. And to show you what a great guy I am, I would even let you take those sweaters off in my bedroom, if you wanted."

She laughed. "Wow. That's very generous of you."

This was what he had missed—what he had never really known. This laughter and tenderness, this binding of his heart to hers. It seemed perfect and easy and absolutely right.

He kissed her once more, wishing they could stay here all night wrapped together by the fire and the Christmas tree while the storm raged outside.

"I meant what I said earlier," she said a long time later. "I love you and I love the boys. I wasn't expecting it, but you McKinley men are pretty hard to resist."

"We do our best," he drawled.

His sons would be over the moon to know their not-so-subtle matchmaking had paid off. He hoped that didn't set a dangerous precedent. Maybe he should warn Jax he had better watch out, or they might turn their attention to him next.

On second thought, Jax was a big boy. He could fend for himself.

He gazed down at her, unable to believe she was really here in his arms. He would never need another Christmas gift as long as he lived. This moment, this night, this woman were beyond his wildest dreams.

He turned serious, compelled to tell her a small portion of what was in his heart. "I love you, Ella. I hope you know that. I wasn't expecting it, either, but nothing has ever felt so right. I love your strength and your courage. I love how sweet you are with my sons. I love that you sacrificed to come back to Pine Gulch and take care of your father, though he's given you nothing but grief in return."

He kissed her again, his heart overflowing with joy and wonder and gratitude. "Most of all, I love that whenever you're near me, I could swear I hear music."

She gave that slow, tender smile he was quickly coming to crave, wrapped her arms around him and let the song carry both of them away.

Epilogue

"I don't know how you did it, but somehow that show was even bigger and better than last year's," Ella's father said as Beck drove away from The Christmas Ranch after her third successful Christmas show in a row.

"You'd better dial it back a bit, babe," her husband said, with that teasing smile she adored. "Everybody's got such high expectations now, you're going to find yourself having to throw a Broadway-quality production in order to meet them."

"I still think last year's show was better," Trevor said from the back seat. "This year Colt and me didn't even get to sing a duet together."

"No, but you played your guitar while all your friends sang 'We Three Kings,'" she answered. "You guys brought down the house, kiddo."

"We were awesome, weren't we?" he said, with that complete lack of humility that always made her smile.

"Hey, Grandpa Curt, what was your favorite part this year?" Colt asked.

Ella knew it always tickled her dad when the boys called him Grandpa Curt, as they had taken to doing since her and Beck's wedding over the summer.

They still usually called her Ella, but had recently asked if she would mind if they called her Mom once in a while. She still teared up every time they did.

As she listened to the twins chatter away to her father, Ella leaned back in the seat and closed her eyes, a wave of fatigue washing over her. The adrenaline rush of finishing a performance was always exhausting, but this seemed to be hitting her harder than usual.

She knew why. After two weeks of achy breasts, mild nausea in the mornings and this unusual fatigue, she'd taken a drugstore test that morning that confirmed her suspicions.

She still hadn't told Beck yet. She was trying to figure out exactly how. Maybe she would wait until Christmas Eve and tell him during their own private celebrations after everyone was in bed and the house was quiet.

Or maybe she would do it tonight. She didn't know how to contain this joy that bubbled through her.

However she told him, she knew Beck would be as happy as she was about adding to their family.

As he drove them toward home, he reached for her hand and brought it to his mouth. He was a big, tough rancher, but every once in a while he did these sweet, spontaneous gestures that completely swept her off her feet.

"You've had quite a day."

She smiled, eyes still closed. "Quite a year, actually."

"It has been amazing, hasn't it?"

Amazing was an understatement. A year ago, she never would have believed her life could be filled with this much joy.

Somehow they were making it work. Shortly after the New Year, her father had finally come to his senses— persuaded in large part by Beck, she knew—and started giving her more and more responsibility at the Baker's Dozen. As of now, she and Curt were comanaging the ranch. She envisioned a day when she and Beck would merge the two operations, as her father intended, but for now the system worked.

She still taught at the elementary school but had surrendered her middle school choir to another teacher.

She even had a small but growing herd of alpacas. The first breeding pair had been Beck's surprise wedding gift to her and she had added three more since then, plus the new offspring of the first pair. She adored them all and had become obsessed with learning all she could about alpaca husbandry.

"Hey, remember last year, when we had that big storm?" Colter said.

"Yeah, and we slid into the ditch and had to wait while you went for help?" Trevor added.

Her journey through the storm had become something of a family legend. Creampuff had earned crab apples for life because of her heroic rescue. Ella still rode her often, as well as the younger, more energetic mare she and Beck had picked out.

"There's the spot, right there," Curt said.

Though it had been a harrowing experience, Ella always smiled when she passed this spot. It had been such a pivotal moment in her life, she would have liked to put a little commemorative plaque on a nearby tree.

A short time later, they pulled up to the ranch house of the Baker's Dozen.

"Can we go see the cria while we're here?" Colter asked.

Cria was the official word for an alpaca baby and her new one was the most adorable thing in the world.

Her father complained the animals were a waste of space, but she couldn't count the number of times she'd caught him sitting by their paddock, just watching them play.

"Sure. Check their water for me while you're there, okay?"

The boys raced off through the cold night to the barn, where the alpaca sheltered in cold weather.

"Let's get you inside," Beck said to her father.

As he helped her father out of the truck, her heart seemed to sigh inside her chest. Every time she saw him offer this kind of patient, gentle care for her father, she fell in love all over again.

Curt's health issues had been the one gray cloud in what had otherwise been a year overflowing with happiness. He was trying a new medicine, though, and so far it seemed to be slowing the progression of his Parkinson's and even reducing some of his trembling.

She knew it was a temporary improvement, but she would take whatever bright spot she could.

The lights were on in the house, which meant Manny and Alina had made it home before them. The ranch foreman and his wife had moved into the big house shortly after Ella's marriage, along with Alina's older brother, Frank. Between the three of them, they took amazing care of Curt and he seemed to enjoy their company.

At some point, she anticipated that her father would

end up moving into the Broken Arrow ranch house with them. He spent much of his time there, anyway, and having him closer would make it easier for her to keep an eye on him. For now, he treasured whatever small portion of independence he still had, and she tried to facilitate that as much as she could.

Now, she saw the Christmas lights were on inside and the Baker's Dozen ranch house was warm and welcoming.

"I'd better go make sure the boys don't try to ruin their good shoes," Beck said after he helped Curt inside.

"I can help you into your room, Dad," she said.

For the next few moments, she was busy easing his swollen feet out of the boots he insisted on wearing and taking off his coat.

"Manny or Frank can help me with the rest," he said.

"All right. I'm glad you came with us, Dad."

"So am I. It really was a great show."

She smiled. "Thanks. I'll be by first thing in the morning to meet with the vet."

Her father tilted his head and gave her a considering look. "You know you're not going to be able to juggle everything when you have that grandbaby of mine, don't you?"

She stared. "How did you know?"

His eyes widened for just a moment, then his expression shifted to a smirk. "You make a poor poker player, honey. That was just a lucky guess—or maybe wishful thinking on my part—but you just confirmed it."

"Don't say anything to Beck," she pleaded. "I haven't told him yet."

"I won't say a word," he promised, then paused. "You picked a good man, Ella."

She smiled. "You don't have to tell me that, Dad. I'll see you in the morning. And don't forget, we have the McRavens' annual party tomorrow night, remember?"

"You ask me, this town has too many damn parties," her father grumbled, though she knew he enjoyed every one of them.

"Good night. Love you."

When she returned to the living room, Beck and the boys had all come back inside and sat in the glow of the Christmas tree they had all decorated here a few Sundays ago. The twins were telling him a story about one of their friends and he nodded solemnly, his gorgeous, masculine features intense as he listened.

As she watched the three of them, her heart couldn't contain all the joy.

Her life was everything she might have wished for and so much more. She had a husband she adored and two stepsons who filled her world with laughter and Legos and tight hugs. She had music and horses, her father, her friends and now this new little life growing inside her.

This was the season of miracles and she would always be grateful for her own—and it had all started with a song.

* * * * *

If you loved this book, be sure to catch up with the Nichols sisters, Hope, Celeste and Faith, in the latest heartwarming holiday stories in
THE COWBOYS OF COLD CREEK
miniseries:

THE HOLIDAY GIFT
(Faith's story)

A COLD CREEK CHRISTMAS STORY
(Celeste's story)

THE CHRISTMAS RANCH
(Hope's story)

Available now wherever Harlequin Special Edition books and ebooks are sold!

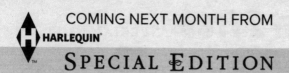

Available November 21, 2017

#2587 MARRIED TILL CHRISTMAS
The Bravos of Justice Creek • by Christine Rimmer
Nell Bravo had her heart broken twice by Declan McGrath; she's not giving him another chance. But Declan has never forgotten her, and when they end up married in Vegas, he's determined to make it work. She'll give him until Christmas, but that's it. Will Declan be able to win her heart before December 26?

#2588 THE MAVERICK'S MIDNIGHT PROPOSAL
Montana Mavericks: The Great Family Roundup • by Brenda Harlen
Rancher Luke Stockton has been estranged from his family for a decade, and now that he's been welcomed home, local baker Eva Rose Armstrong warms his heart with her home-baked goods—but is he worthy of her love?

#2589 YULETIDE BABY BARGAIN
Return to the Double C • by Allison Leigh
When a two-month-old baby is left on Lincoln Swift's doorstep, the Wyoming oilman can think of only one thing to do—call old "friend" Maddie Templeton to come to the rescue. The next thing they know, they're caring for baby Layla and living together in Linc's home. But between the Christmas spirit and their strong attraction, this baby bargain might just result in love!

#2590 CHRISTMASTIME COURTSHIP
Matchmaking Mamas • by Marie Ferrarella
The Matchmaking Mamas are at it again, and this time they've arranged for Miranda Steele to get a speeding ticket from none other than Colin Kirby, a brooding motorcycle cop. He's determined to maintain his loner status, but can he resist Miranda's sunny charm and Christmas cheer?

#2591 A FORTUNES OF TEXAS CHRISTMAS
The Fortunes of Texas • by Helen Lacey
It's Christmas in Texas and another secret Fortune is coming home! Amersen Beaudin has left France to answer the summons of Kate Fortune, but when he meets lovely landscaper Robin Harbin, sparks fly. As Christmas approaches, can Amersen come to terms with his new family and own up to his love for Robin?

#2592 SLEIGH BELLS IN CRIMSON
Crimson, Colorado • by Michelle Major
Lucy is determined to get her life on track, and the town of Crimson, along with rough-around-the-edges rancher Caden Sharpe, soon become an important part of that. Her feisty spirit might be just what Caden needs to heal his emotional wounds. But when her past comes back to haunt them both, will their love be strong enough to weather the storm?

YOU CAN FIND MORE INFORMATION ON UPCOMING HARLEQUIN® TITLES, FREE EXCERPTS AND MORE AT WWW.HARLEQUIN.COM.

HSECNM1117

Get 2 Free Books,

Plus 2 Free Gifts—

just for trying the

Reader Service!

SPECIAL EXCERPT FROM

H HARLEQUIN®

SPECIAL EDITION

*He may have broken her heart twice,
but Declan McGrath has never forgotten Nell Bravo,
and when they end up married in Vegas, he's determined
to make it work. She'll give him until Christmas, but
that's it. Will Declan be able to win her heart before
December 26?*

Read on for a sneak preview of
MARRIED TILL CHRISTMAS,
the final book in New York Times *bestselling author*
Christine Rimmer's *beloved miniseries*
THE BRAVOS OF JUSTICE CREEK.

"Why me—and why won't you take a hint that I'm just not interested?"

He stared into his single malt, neat, as if the answer to her question waited in the smoky amber depths. "I don't believe you're not interested. You just don't trust me."

"Duh." She poured on the sarcasm and made a big show of tapping a finger against her chin. "Let me think. I wonder why?"

"How many times do I need to say that I messed up? I messed up twice. I'm so damn sorry and I need you to forgive me. You're the best thing that ever happened to me. And…" He shook his head. "Fine. I get it. I smashed your heart to tiny, bloody bits. How many ways can I say I was wrong?"

Okay. He was kind of getting to her. For a second there, she'd almost reached across the table and touched his clenched fist. She so had to watch herself. Gently she suggested, "How about this? I accept your apology. It was years ago and we need to move on."

He slanted her a sideways look, dark brows showing

glints of auburn in the light from above. "Yeah?"

"Yeah."

"So then we can try again?"

Should she have known that would be his next question? Yeah, probably. "I didn't say that."

"I want another chance."

"Well, that's not happening."

"Yes, it is. And when it does, I'm not letting you go. This time it's going to be forever."

She almost grinned. Because that was another thing about Deck. Not only did he have big arms, broad shoulders and a giant brain.

He was cocky. Very, very cocky.

And she was enjoying herself far too much. It really was a whole lot of fun to argue with him. It always had been. And the most fun of all was finally being the one in the position of power.

Back when they'd been together, he was the poor kid and she was a Bravo—one of the Bastard Bravos, as everybody had called her mother's children behind their backs. But a Bravo, nonetheless. Nell always had the right clothes and a certain bold confidence that made her popular. She hadn't been happy at home by any stretch, but guys had wanted to go out with her and girls had kind of envied her.

And all she'd ever wanted was Deck. So, really, he'd had all the power then.

Now, for some reason she didn't really understand, he'd decided he just had to get another chance with her. Now she was the one saying no. Payback was a bitch, all right. Not to mention downright delicious.

Don't miss
MARRIED TILL CHRISTMAS by Christine Rimmer,
available December 2017 wherever
Harlequin® Special Edition books and ebooks are sold.

New York Times bestselling author

brenda novak

returns to Silver Springs with a moving story about rebuilding your life when you've got nothing left to lose...

Savanna Gray needs a do-over. Her "perfect" life unraveled when, to her absolute shock, her husband was arrested for attacking three women. With her divorce settled, she takes her two children to Silver Springs to seek refuge between the walls of a farmhouse her late father had planned to renovate.

Gavin Turner understands the struggle of starting over. He was abandoned at a gas station when he was five, and it wasn't until he landed at New Horizons Boys Ranch as a teen that he finally found some peace. He steps up when Savanna needs help fixing things—even when those things go beyond the farmhouse.

Despite an escalating attraction to Gavin, Savanna resolves to keep her distance, unwilling to repeat her past mistakes. But it's hard to resist a man whose heart is as capable as his hands.

Available now, wherever books are sold!